Ross took another step toward her

"Keep away! I don't want you to touch me."

Unconsciously Ginny rubbed at her cheek where his fingers had caressed it, as if trying to erase the imprint of his touch. She knew what this man was, yet for a brief space of time, she'd been weak enough to succumb to his seductive expertise.

His hateful smile surfaced again, the light of mockery that gleamed in the blue depths of his eyes, incensing her. "I said, I don't want you near me."

"My, we do overreact to one little touch, don't we?" Ross said. "And as for keeping my distance, I'm afraid that will be difficult—because you see, I intend that you'll be sharing my bed for the rest of the night."

Kate Walker chose the Brontë sisters, the development of their writing from childhood to maturity, as the topic for her master's thesis. It is little wonder, then, that she should go on to write romance fiction. She lives in the United Kingdom with her husband and son, and when she isn't writing, she tries to keep up with her hobbies of embroidery, knitting, antiques and, of course, reading.

Books by Kate Walker

KATE WALKER

leap in the dark

Harlequin Books

TORONTO • NEW YORK • LONDON
AMSTERDAM • PARIS • SYDNEY • HAMBURG
STOCKHOLM • ATHENS • TOKYO • MILAN

For Ruth

Harlequin Presents first edition May 1990
ISBN 0-373-11269-6

Original hardcover edition published in 1989
by Mills & Boon Limited

CHAPTER ONE

HER head hurt. That was the first thought that came to Ginny as she stirred restlessly, lying in that half-way stage between sleeping and waking—because at this point she believed she had been asleep. At first she thought that the ache filled the whole of her face, but then, slowly, it centred on one spot on the right-hand side of her jaw, a nagging, throbbing sensation that had her burying her head in the pillows with a groan.

Pillows. The word penetrated the heavy fog that clouded her brain and, still with her eyes closed, she moved her hand upwards, feeling the softness of feathers under the crisp cotton. If she had been asleep it was only natural that her head should be resting on a pillow, but for some reason that seemed wrong, disturbingly so, and in the hazy recesses of her thoughts she had a vague recollection of another moment of coming close to waking, surfacing from the depths of dark unconsciousness, to find that she was lying, uncomfortably curled up, on something that was harder than a bed, smelt of leather and—she frowned at the unexpected memory—that swayed and bounced occasionally as if it were moving.

'Don't talk rubbish!'

She muttered the words out loud; they seemed more convincing that way. The memory was too incredible to be true; it had to be a dream, she told herself, though at the back of her mind was the worrying thought that there was something she should remember, something connected with that hazy recollection, something that sent a quiver of unease through her, though when she tried to grasp at it it eluded her, sliding away into nothingness.

It was time she woke up, she decided; time she left such dreams behind. It must be well near time to get up and get ready for work—already the sun was shining brightly on her face. It took an unusual effort to open her eyes; normally she snapped wide awake minutes before the alarm went off, but this morning her head seemed thick and heavy.

I'd better get an early night tonight, Ginny decided, forcing her eyes open. Then every trace of sleepiness fled from her mind as she found herself staring in shock and blank horror at a room she had never seen before in her life.

'No!'

All colour drained from her cheeks, and she sat upright with a jolt that made her head spin. Opposite the bed was a dressing-table with a tall mirror, and Ginny caught sight of her own reflection in the glass, staring at it for a long moment as if to reassure herself that she was still herself, that she hadn't somehow been transformed into another person, as alien to her as this unknown room.

She knew a sense of relief at the realisation that at least she was fully dressed, her neat white blouse and navy skirt rather crumpled from the way she had been lying, and, reassuringly familiar, her own face stared back at her. Oval-shaped, with widely spaced brown eyes under dark brows, a long mouth with full, softly pink lips, all topped with a profusion of dark auburn curls, it was a face that was interesting rather than pretty. No one could ever call her beautiful; 'striking' was the highest compliment she had ever been paid.

Normally her skin had plenty of colour, but with the shock of discovering that she had no idea where she was her cheeks had become ashen white, and against the pale skin, low down on her jaw, a dark shadow of a bruise showed clearly. With tentative fingers Ginny touched the spot delicately, wincing at the pain caused by even such a gentle pressure, and from the whirl of confusion in her mind an image surfaced, a picture of a darkly hostile masculine face, a pair of icy blue eyes and a cold, curt voice saying, 'Then I'm afraid you leave me with no alternative.'

Desperately Ginny shook her head, trying to clear it so that she could think. *Where* was she? How had she got here? Wide and dark with panic, her eyes swept round the room again.

Decorated in soft tones of blue and grey, with an array of built-in wardrobes and a thick smoke-coloured carpet, it was an attractive, comfortable room, but one she had never seen before in her life. She was sure she would have remembered it if she had ever been here before. So what was she doing here? How—*who* had brought her here? Had that man—?

Ginny tried to focus her thoughts on the dark, blue-eyed man, but the image had faded and she couldn't bring it clearly to mind. Her head ached with the effort; the silence in the room seemed to grow more oppressive with each moment that passed, and fear tied her stomach muscles in tight, painful knots. Then her eyes went to the window and she roused herself to action. Perhaps outside, beyond the glass, she would see something that would give her a clue as to where she was. Swinging her feet to the ground, she stood up, then reached for the bedhead with a gasp as her head swam and she feared she might fall.

Once more her eyes went to her reflection and the bruise on her face. She must have hurt herself somehow, but she had no recollection of a fall or anything else that might have caused the injury. Was that what had happened? Had she fallen, fainted or somehow knocked herself out? And had someone picked her up and brought her here?

But where *was* here? Determination to see what was beyond the window overcame her weakness, and with wavering, unsteady steps, her hands outstretched, ready to support her if necessary, she made her way slowly across the room.

Her sense of triumph at reaching the window was drowned under a wave of disappointment as she looked out at a garden that was as unfamiliar to her as the room in which she had found herself. Carefully tended lawns stretched away towards a thick beech hedge, and beyond that hedge there was no sign of any habitation, no house or shops to give her a clue, only green fields and a single, winding road. There was nothing familiar about it and, worst of all, no one to whom she could call, ask for help, or at least an explanation.

With a despondent sigh Ginny sank down on a nearby chair, struggling to get her incoherent thoughts into some sort of order. Her eyes fell on her handbag lying on the dressing-table, and with a cry of joy she reached for it, disproportionately delighted to see at least one familiar object in this alien, nightmarish world. A hasty examination of its contents soon told her that nothing was missing, that small fact bringing a swift rush of relief. At least she hadn't been mugged, attacked in the street and robbed. But she had to find out what had happened. Her next move would have to be to open the bedroom door and venture out. Perhaps there was someone downstairs...

The fuzzy feeling in her head had cleared slightly, and she made the brief journey rather more steadily, though she was thankful when she finally came to a halt, leaning against the door for a moment to get her breath back. Another few moments and the whole puzzle would be solved; there was bound to be a perfectly rational explanation. But when she tried to turn the doorhandle all her fears came back with a rush as her efforts met with stubborn resistance and the door refused to budge.

'Open, damn you!' Ginny muttered, a rising note of desperation in her voice as she pulled frantically at the recalcitrant handle. '*Please* open!'

But her efforts were to no avail, and her legs suddenly felt like cotton wool beneath her so that she sank to the floor, a sob rising in her throat at the realisation that the door was well and truly locked.

'Help! Oh, help!'

Her voice was weak, quavering noticeably as fear swamped her. If only she could remember!

Just then a tiny noise reached her from the floor below. It was very faint, just the sound of a door opening, but it spurred her into action. Getting to her feet, she balled her hands into fists and pounded against the door, heedless of the bruises she inflicted on herself.

'Let me out! Let me out! Do you hear me? You can't keep me locked up like this! Let me out!'

Pausing for breath, she listened hard. Silence. Had anyone heard her? Then, just as she lifted her hands to bang at the door again, she heard another sound, one that froze her movements, leaving her standing transfixed.

Footsteps, slow, unhurried footsteps, climbing the stairs. Heavy footsteps, not a child's or a woman's. Her stomach lurched queasily. She had been determined to get a response, but now she was no longer sure she wanted to know who was on the other side of the door.

Unable to move, she heard a key turn in the lock and watched as if hypnotised as the door slowly opened.

'There was no need to try to break the door down,' a man's voice said on a note of mockery that jarred her already raw nerves. She had heard that voice before, but her mind was so blurred and confused with stress that she couldn't put a face to it.

'I——' she began indignantly, but then another sound from downstairs floated upwards, unexpected and thoroughly disturbing in the memories it evoked. A child's laughter. Dear heaven, she had forgotten Jamie and Lisa!

The door had opened fully and, as her brown eyes met a pair of coldly amused blue ones, all other thoughts fled from her mind. She had a confused impression of a strong, rangy frame, powerful shoulders that to her hypersensitive mind seemed almost to fill the doorway in which the man stood, and a hard, cruel-looking mouth and determined jaw. As her eyes went back to those blue, blue eyes, her face became ashen with shock.

'*You!*'

It came out as a shaken gasp, because as soon as she had seen his face she had remembered.

Gavin Marshall had come to the agency on the worst possible day. One typewriter was on the blink, three of Ginny's most reliable workers had rung in sick, victims of a particularly virulent dose of flu that was rapidly reaching epidemic proportions in the small town of

Epton, and the decorators who had been booked for the following week had turned up a week early, insisting that they had to start work now or not at all.

Driven into a small corner of her office, surrounded by dustsheets and paintpots, Ginny had been involved in a particularly difficult telephone call to the employer of one of the sick women when she looked up to see a tall, strikingly handsome blond man manoeuvring his way past the boiler-suited workmen with a careful concern for the elegant and clearly expensive dark brown suit that was tailored to his slim frame.

'Yes, Mrs Baker, someone will be round within the hour, you have my word on that.'

With a sigh of relief she put the phone down and turned to the man before her with a smile.

'Domestic Help?' he asked, consulting a card he had pulled out of his pocket. 'I'm looking for a Miss Fletcher.'

'That's right. I'm Virginia Fletcher.'

Her proffered hand was taken briefly in a limp, reluctant grip that she instinctively disliked. Experience had taught her that such an insincere handshake came from the sort of person she wouldn't like at all. But she wouldn't have to work with this man. When this interview was finished, she probably wouldn't have anything further to do with him.

'Won't you sit down?'

Hastily she twitched a grubby dustsheet from the nearest chair and watched as he lowered himself gingerly into it, adjusting the creases in his immaculate trousers and the set of his jacket with a careful precision.

'How can I help you, Mr——?'

'Marshall, Gavin Marshall. I've just moved into Epton, I bought the Meridew house. I expect you know it?'

Ginny nodded. Everyone knew the Meridew house, and the fact that it had recently been sold for some staggering sum—to someone with more money than sense, her mother had commented, and privately Ginny was inclined to agree with her. Imposing and luxurious it might be, but it was far too modern for her taste. Ugly and soulless was the way she would have described it, but, of course, she wasn't going to admit that to its new owner.

'Were you looking for a housekeeper, Mr Marshall?'

That was what most of the people who used her agency wanted—a housekeeper or a good, reliable cleaner, or sometimes a childminder. Just recently there had been an increase in the number of young married women looking for someone to care for their children while they went to work, which showed the way the character of Epton was changing from its rather old-fashioned 'county' image as a result of a much-needed influx of new employers into it.

'A housekeeper, yes.'

The fair head inclined in agreement, and a waft of some over-heavy aftershave reached Ginny's nostrils, so that she had to fight against the urge to wrinkle her nose in distaste. Mentally she was already checking through the women on her books, trying to think of someone who would be suitable for this particular post. Clearly Gavin Marshall had plenty of money. His clothes, that overpowering aftershave, a gleaming gold watch on his wrist and everything about his manner spoke of wealth and a liking for an ornate sort of style. 'Flash' was how she would have described him, her mother's words echoing inside her head.

A few pertinent questions narrowed the field down, and as they discussed arrangements for the interviews she would set up Ginny thought she already knew exactly who he would choose. Nancy Hayes would be just right—and she wouldn't consider Mr Marshall flash at all. In fact, she would probably fall for him at first sight. Hastily she dragged her attention back to the matter in hand as she realised that Gavin Marshall had moved on to another topic.

'And then there's the question of the children.'

Children? Privately, Ginny admitted to some surprise. Gavin Marshall didn't strike her as the paternal type at all. He was clearly a man who was going places. He had consulted that expensive watch three times already during the brief interview, his action seeming to imply that his time was too precious to waste sitting here. Also, his appearance was rather too perfect. He had none of the slightly dishevelled look that characterised Sam, her brother-in-law, who was the father of two small boys and loved every minute of it.

'There's Jamie—he's six—and Lisa who's four and a half. They'll both be going to Holme Hall.' He named the exclusive, fee-paying school ten miles away from Epton. 'I leave for work at eight, so I'll need someone to take them to school in the mornings and bring them back at the end of the day. After that, the housekeeper can look after them.'

Nancy Hayes wasn't going to like that, Ginny thought, reconsidering her list of potential housekeepers. She had no liking for children at all. Ginny felt a pang of sympathy for the unknown Jamie and Lisa, left to the care of someone who would very probably resent having to look after them.

'Does Mrs Marshall work, too?' she asked carefully.

For the first time, that mask of suave composure slipped slightly. 'My wife is dead.'

'Oh, I'm sorry,' Ginny apologised hastily. 'I didn't know.'

'Of course not—how could you? It was in America—the children have been living there for the last year.'

An odd turn of phrase, Ginny reflected, noting that he hadn't said, 'we've been living there.' Perhaps he and his wife had been separated.

'I would need some assurance that whoever does the job wouldn't talk to the children about their mother—ask any awkward questions. They need to forget——'

Wouldn't it be better to let them talk, let it all out? The question hovered on the tip of Ginny's tongue, but she swallowed it down hastily.

'This isn't exactly the sort of thing we usually deal with——'

When she had set up the agency, she had very soon discovered that most of the women she employed wanted jobs that would fit in with the hours their children were at school. Delivering and collecting the Marshall children would involve just the sort of time no one wanted to be tied up, and it would restrict them to being available in a way that would cut into their day, both in the morning and the afternoon.

'I take it there's no relation who could help?'

Gavin shook his head.

'There is an uncle—my wife's brother—but he doesn't live locally. In fact, I've no idea where he's living now—and if I did I wouldn't want him near my kids.'

With some surprise, Ginny noted how the bite of anger had slid into the previously calm and collected voice.

'My brother-in-law is not the sort of person I'd want to care for my children. He and I have never got on.' His tone made it clear that the comment was a strong understatement. 'He was against me from the very start, and he upset my wife with his hostility towards our marriage, until he succeeded in poisoning her mind against me.'

So she had been right, Gavin Marshall's marriage *had* broken up before his wife's death. But what right had his brother-in-law to interfere? Ginny felt a spurt of anger towards the unknown man who had interfered so arrogantly, putting the happiness of two young children at risk.

'Besides, he's not the type to give a damn about Jamie and Lisa.' Gavin was now clearly launched on the subject of his wife's brother, his eyes dark with anger. 'He's the typical bachelor—totally irresponsible—the last I'd heard he'd just thrown up his job and taken off into the country somewhere. And he's an inveterate womaniser.'

Contempt thickened Gavin's tone. 'He goes his own sweet way and doesn't give a damn for anyone else— the sort who'll treat a woman as he does his job—pick it up when it interests him, then drop it without a second thought as soon as something new and interesting comes along. The kids would have a new "aunt" every week if they spent any time with him—and heaven knows what he'd say to them about me. I'd have to be very desperate indeed to ask for his help.'

Ginny felt she could well understand his feelings. This uncle sounded a thoroughly untrustworthy and unpleasant character, certainly not the type to whom she would want to entrust Rory and Jason, her two nephews.

'Don't you think that perhaps a taxi—' she began, then caught herself up hastily, remembering that he had said that the children were only six and four. How would they feel if they were left with a complete stranger, probably a different person each day, during the ten-mile drive to the school?

Sympathy tugged at her heart at the thought of how they must feel, having so recently lost their mother and been brought here from America by a father who, if their parents had been separated, they probably didn't know all that well.

But there was no one on her books who would be likely to want to take the job on—Ginny paused as a sudden thought struck her. The Meridew house wasn't very far from where she lived. She could easily drop the children off at school and still be at her desk for just after nine; and she usually took a coffee-break around three-thirty, anyway.

'We might just be able to manage it.' To her surprise, she found herself speaking before she had fully decided.

'It would only be for a few months. I'm planning on getting married again.'

Ginny was afraid her surprise must have shown on her face. How long ago had his wife died? She had thought it had been recently but, if Gavin Marshall was thinking of remarrying, then perhaps that wasn't the case. Still, if the job was only for a short time, then surely she could manage it?

'Then we'll definitely be able to help you,' she said crisply, pushing to the back of her mind the thought that her father, who was also her accountant, would tear his hair at the way she had, in his opinion, let her feelings get in the way of what he considered to be sound business sense. He had set her up in the agency, providing vital capital needed to obtain an office and all the necessary equipment, and he took a strong interest in her affairs. A hard-headed businessman himself, he was unlikely to understand the impulse that had led her to consider taking on such an awkward and unprofitable commission. They had argued the point before, when in the past she had sometimes reduced her charges or, on one occasion, waived them completely, when she had been approached by pensioners in need of someone to help with housework they could no longer do themselves.

'You'll never make a profit that way!' he had protested.

'I'm making as much profit as I want to,' Ginny had replied. 'And I called the agency Domestic Help because *help* is what I want to provide.'

'Well, you just watch your step, young lady. One of these days, your charitable impulses are going to land you in a very tight spot indeed.'

But that wasn't likely with this particular job, Ginny thought, turning a confident smile on Gavin Marshall.

'I'll transport your children myself, Mr Marshall. If you'll just give me the details of exactly when you want them picked up——'

In the end the arrangement worked out surprisingly well. By taking the quiet country roads that led to the school, Ginny was able to avoid the queues of traffic that built up on the routes into town and arrived at her office very little later than usual, and she soon came to enjoy the break from her desk when she collected the children and took them home. Autumn had always been her favourite time of the year, and, having spent the last eighteen months working non-stop to build up her business, get her name known and acquire a reputation for efficiency and reliability of which she was justifiably proud, she had had little time to enjoy the changing colours and mellow tones she now saw every day, her pleasure in the trips increasing as she slowly got to know the children in her care.

If she had had any doubts about her decision to help Gavin Marshall, they vanished as soon as she saw Jamie and Lisa, their small faces white with nerves as they waited on the steps of the Meridew house on that first morning. Jamie was an exceptionally beautiful child, tall for his age and very slim, with his father's blond hair and bright, amazingly blue eyes, while Lisa was a charming, elf-like creature with the same, clear blue eyes and a shining cap of jet-black hair which, Ginny assumed, could only have come from her mother. Clearly the late Mrs Marshall hadn't shared her husband's fair colouring. Her heart had gone out to the pair of them, they looked so lost and alone—and no wonder, when they had suffered the loss of their mother so young and had then been transported from their home in America to a totally strange house in another country.

At first the children had been painfully shy and reluctant to talk, but slowly Ginny drew them out, and by the third week Lisa at least would chat to her easily during the drive, her light voice with its pronounced American accent recounting the things she had done the previous day. Jamie remained rather more restrained and aloof. As the elder child, Ginny supposed the death of his mother had affected him more than his sister, and once more she questioned Mr Marshall's instructions that no mention was to be made of this event, having to bite her lips hard on several occasions when some remark of the little boy's would have led her naturally to bring up the subject, believing that, deep down, he wanted to talk it out. She took special trouble to try and get to know him, helped by a lucky chance discovery of his passion for swimming—a sport she greatly enjoyed herself—which gave them a shared interest to discuss and broke down some of the barriers.

By the third week they had fallen into an easy routine and Ginny found herself looking forward to the time she spent with her two young charges, particularly when the Wednesday morning turned out to be the sort of beautiful day that an English autumn could produce, with clear blue skies and a warm sun which made the weather appear almost summer-like.

Lisa was chattering away about the papier-mâché head she had made at school the day before, and Ginny would hardly have noticed Jamie's silence if she hadn't glanced in her mirror and seen how, contrary to her instructions, he had unfastened his seat-belt and was kneeling up on the back seat, staring out of the window.

'Jamie,' she said in quiet warning; then, as he ignored her, 'Jamie, sit down properly,' she added more firmly.

For a moment she thought he wasn't going to obey her, behaviour so uncharacteristic that it made her wonder just what had caught his attention, and she had opened her mouth to add a second, more forceful reproof when, obviously reluctant, he twisted round and slid down into his seat, glancing at his sister as he did so.

'It *is*——' he began in an urgent undertone, but the rest of what he had been about to say was lost in the roar of an engine as the dark blue Escort which had been following them closely for the last couple of miles suddenly swung out to overtake them and disappeared at a speed that Ginny found positively foolhardy on such a narrow, winding road.

'Road hog!' she muttered under her breath, with a furious glare at the back of the driver's black head as she admitted to relief at seeing him go. His closeness had been making her uneasy for a while, and she couldn't understand why he hadn't overtaken before, at some safer point in the road. She glanced back at the children. 'Seat-belt, Jamie,' she reminded him gently, turning her attention back to Lisa as soon as she heard the familiar click that meant the belt was safely fastened.

'And today we're going to paint them,' the little girl was saying. 'Mrs Guthrie says we can make puppets out of them and make up a play like Punch and Judy.'

'What a lovely idea. Have you ever seen a Punch and Judy show, Lisa? Do they have them in America? I remember when I was eight I—oh, damn!'

The involuntary exclamation escaped her as she rounded a particularly difficult bend and then had to slam on the brakes hard as she caught sight of the blue Escort which had passed them earlier and was now stationary but slewed across the road at such an angle that it was impossible for her to pass it on either side.

'Sorry!' she said hastily as the children were jolted in their seats. 'I knew he'd come to grief, driving like that. Some people have no sense! Stay where you are, you two, while I find out what's going on.'

Had he taken that last bend so fast that his car had gone out of control? Or had his car's engine given up on him? she wondered as she released her seat-belt and pushed open the door. Either way, he didn't appear particularly concerned about it; he hadn't even opened the bonnet to see where the problem was, but was lounging nonchalantly against the car, his long body relaxed as if he was simply enjoying the warmth of the sun.

'Is something wrong?'

Later, Ginny was unable to say just why her steps had suddenly halted, why she had hesitated to go any closer. There was nothing particularly aggressive in the man's stance, nothing to bring fear to her mind, but somehow, in the moment that he turned his head to look at her, his eyes narrowed against the sun, some instinct stronger than rational thought sent a prickling sense of warning running through her veins so that the tiny hairs on the back of her neck lifted in the instinctive response of a wary cat faced with an alien and threatening predator.

'Is there some problem with your car?' She tried to iron the uncertainty from her voice, wanting to appear calm and in control of the situation, but in spite of her efforts it rose and fell unevenly, betraying her unease.

Broad shoulders under a battered denim jacket lifted in an indifferent shrug.

'I don't know,' he said with a wry, lop-sided smile.

That smile would charm the birds out of the trees, Ginny admitted privately to herself, the hypersensitive tingle of her nerves lulled momentarily under an involuntary acknowledgement of the physical appeal of a tanned, strong-boned face with a firm, determined jaw, and jet-black hair that was unexpectedly fine and soft if the way it had fallen forward as he turned his head was anything to go by.

'Do you know anything about engines?'

The question came quite innocently, but as Ginny met the apparently frank, open gaze of a pair of vivid eyes, so blue that they seemed a reflection of the clear, bright sky above, she felt a sudden shiver of apprehension run down her spine as if the sun had been hidden behind a cloud.

Charming as it had been, that smile was not genuine. There had been a coldness, a withdrawal in the man's eyes that worried her, making her uncomfortably aware of the fact that he was a powerfully built character with a broad chest and shoulders, and that she and the children were alone with him in this deserted country road. As the man straightened up to his full height, she watched him warily, her muscles tensing.

'Perhaps you could have a look at it.'

'I'm no mechanic!' Ginny's response came tartly. This show of apparent ignorance didn't fit at all with the external image the man presented. He looked strong, forceful, and eminently capable of coping with any problem that came his way. So why was he feigning complete ignorance about his car?

Or perhaps she was over-reacting. Assuming that any man was well-versed in the workings of a car's engine was as sexist an opinion as believing that every woman knew how to sew—which she couldn't, not even to save her life. And the hands that now rested against the dark bonnet of the car didn't look as if they were accustomed to hard physical work, being clean and well cared for, with no calluses or broken nails. So perhaps the innocence was not just show. With a small shake she pulled herself together.

'I only know the basics, but I'll have a look if you like,' she went on in a more reasonable tone, although she was unable to suppress the reluctance that shaded her voice. Dressed for work as she was, she wasn't keen on running the risk that her smart navy suit, worn with a crisp white blouse, would end up stained with oil.

'I'd appreciate that.'

He made a move as if to open the car bonnet, but as Ginny came closer she saw his eyes flick to her face, then past her towards her own car. Instinctively she turned, catching Jamie in the act of scrambling out of the car.

'Stay in the car!' she called hastily, nervousness sharpening her tone as her words clashed with something the little boy was saying, making it inaudible. 'Jamie, go back.'

Automatically she took a step towards him with the intention of bundling him back into the car. His appearance had suddenly brought home to her the recollection of how wealthy Jamie's father was, which brought with it a whole new set of explanations for this man being here, blocking their way like this, other than the purely accidental one she had first assumed, reviving those disturbing anxieties all over again.

'Jamie, I said—oh!'

The words broke off on a cry of shock and alarm as hard fingers closed around her wrist, jerking her to a halt with an abrupt force that almost pulled her off her feet. Anger driving away her natural caution, she swung round, yellow fires of fury flaring in her brown eyes.

'Just what do you think you're doing? Let me go at once!'

His silent, stony-faced shake of the head had her mouth drying in apprehension and fear, and it was an effort to force the next words through stiff, dry lips.

'I said, let go! I have to take these children to school——'

'Ginny——'

It was Jamie's voice from behind her, and as he spoke she saw the man's face change, setting into hard, cold lines that twisted something painfully deep inside her. Struggling for composure, she ignored Jamie's interruption, nerving herself to meet those electric blue eyes that were now frighteningly cold, with something that looked like scathing contempt turning them to icy steel.

'And we're late already,' she blundered on, her mind refusing to accept what was happening—what she was afraid was happening. 'If you could just move your car out of the way so that we can get past, I'll contact a garage as soon as I've dropped the children off and someone will come out...'

Her voice faltered, died as nothing she said altered that stony, implacable gaze. He had to have the coldest eyes she had ever seen, Ginny thought, struggling to keep a grip on herself. How could she ever have thought this man even remotely attractive—and what *was* he going to do with them? Her control snapping, she pulled hard at his restraining hand.

'Don't panic.'

The calm voice did nothing to restore her confidence; on the contrary, its cool control had exactly the opposite effect, setting her heart thudding, so that she found it impossible to breathe naturally, her racing pulse making her head swim.

'I'm not going to hurt you.' The steely tone penetrated the whirling haze that filled her mind. 'It's not you I want—just the kids.'

'Never!'

The word sprang from her lips in the same second that a series of terrifying images formed in her mind. She could see it all now: Gavin Marshall's wealth—the big house—two children following an exact routine for weeks—with only herself for protection.

The peaceful quiet of the early morning became suddenly fraught with tension and fear. This was no simple accident, no unlucky breakdown, but a deliberate ambush, the man before her no unfortunate motorist, but a kidnapper—someone who must have observed every move they made, watched them over the past weeks and planned every move with care.

Why had she never noticed him before? He must have followed them to discover their route, must have chosen just this particular spot for the way it was so very iso-lated—exactly half-way between two tiny villages and surrounded by woodland on both sides, not a house for miles. And, as Ginny knew from her regular trips to and from the school, the chances of another car passing this way were almost nil.

'I just want the children.'

Ginny shivered at the menace in the man's voice, and an icy hand seemed to grip her heart at the thought of what he might do if she resisted. But she couldn't just hand over Jamie and Lisa without a fight. They had been through enough already in their young lives; she couldn't abandon them, leave them alone and terrified in this man's hands.

'If you'll just tell them to come over here——'

'No!'

The single syllable rang sharply through the still air and, although Ginny quailed inside at the black frown that crossed the man's face, she forced herself to meet those hateful eyes with what she hoped was a fair degree of equanimity.

'Those children are in my care, and if you think——'

'I don't think,' he cut in sharply, 'I know. The children are the ones I want—I've no quarrel with you. If you'll just hand them over, you can go on your way without any worries.'

'No worries?'

Once more Ginny fought to free herself from the hard grip on her wrist that was now becoming distinctly uncomfortable. Her impotent struggles only resulted in a tightening of his grasp until she winced with pain.

'*No worries?*' she repeated, her voice rising in a mixture of fear and anger. 'Do you really think I wouldn't *worry* if I did as you said, and left Jamie and Lisa alone with a—an animal like you? I could never live with myself if I did.'

Just for one second she almost believed she had disconcerted him. The cold blue eyes narrowed briefly and the swift glance that he shot her had a new, keenly assessing quality. But if he was taken aback it was only for a moment, and before she could use the tiny advantage he spoke again.

'I'll give you one last chance, lady. Tell Jamie and Lisa to get out of the car and come over here, and I'll let you go. Otherwise, I won't be answerable for the consequences.'

It took every ounce of courage that Ginny possessed to ignore the threat that laced the quietly savage voice. Swallowing hard, she drew herself up, glaring defiance into his granite-hard face.

'I said no and I meant *no!*'

'Then I'm afraid you leave me with no alternative——'

His movement towards her terrified Ginny, her mind hazing with panic as she twisted frantically, her feet in high-heeled shoes slipping on the surface of the road. She knew a moment of despair as she realised that she was falling, felt an agonising pain in her jaw, and then everything went completely black.

CHAPTER TWO

'You!'

Shock, consternation and a wave of sheer blind fury drove the weakness from Ginny's limbs, and without a thought for the wisdom of her actions she launched herself straight at the figure in the doorway, one hand uplifted to strike that mocking smile from his face.

But the blow never made contact. With an insultingly lazy move he reached out and caught her wrist in a bruising grip, neatly sidestepping to avoid the savage kick she aimed at his ankles.

'Behave yourself!' The command came in a low voice, but one forceful enough to stop Ginny in her tracks, her furious brown eyes clashing with his cool blue ones so that she could almost imagine she could see sparks in the air.

'Behave?' she spluttered angrily. '*Behave?* Who are you to speak of *behaving*? What sort of behaviour is it to kidnap two small children and take them heaven knows where?'

Broad shoulders under a blue checked cotton shirt as well-worn as the denim jacket he had had on earlier lifted in an indifferent shrug.

'I have my reasons.'

'Oh, I'm sure you have!' That unemotional voice incensed Ginny. What sort of callous monster could be so coldly indifferent to the fear and distress he was inflicting on two young children? 'And all of them measured in hundreds of pounds, I've no doubt! What has Gavin Marshall done to you?'

Those blue eyes looked straight into hers, not a flicker of emotion in their clear depths.

'To me personally—nothing,' he said calmly, and it was the frankness of that 'nothing' that broke Ginny's tenuous hold on her self-control.

'You bastard!'

Her free hand flew up, aiming straight at his face, but her action was as impotent as it had been before. Her captor simply lifted an arm up before his face and her fist collided with hard bone and sinewy muscle with a force that had her crying out in pain and shock.

'Show some sense, woman!' For the first time, genuine emotion showed in the man's voice. He sounded as if he was having difficulty holding on to his temper, and the repressed violence of his tone sent shivers of fear running down Ginny's spine. 'I don't want to hurt you!'

'You already have.'

The words slid out weakly. Ginny's hand ached where it had slammed against his arm, and her head felt cloudy and unfocused, the bruise on her chin throbbing painfully as the strength anger had given her died away and she was swamped by a huge wave of desolation at the realisation that her puny attempts at defiance had had no effect at all on this man.

'You did that to yourself.' That cold, quiet voice lanced through the mists that were clouding her mind like a spear of ice. 'You——' He broke off abruptly, and when he spoke again Ginny was frankly stunned to catch a note of what sounded amazingly like concern in his voice. 'Are you all right?'

Oh, how she longed to defy him again, to declare that she was fine, never better, but the words wouldn't form on a tongue that seemed strangely thick and clumsy. She couldn't see clearly and, as she gropingly reached out a hand for support, she felt it taken in a firm, warm grasp that was so very different from the cruel, punishing grip of only moments before that it rocked her sense of reality.

'I——' she began, then stopped because, to her chagrin, tears were very close and she had no intention of letting him see them.

'You'd better sit down.'

Strong hands supported her, leading her across the room, and Ginny was beyond resisting, moving like a robot until she felt herself being lowered gently on to the bed.

'Put your head between your knees.' Firm pressure on the back of her neck ensured her obedience to his instructions. 'And take some deep breaths.'

She had no alternative but to obey. She was past thinking for herself and, besides, instinctively she knew that his advice was sensible. After a couple of gulping, half-sobbing breaths, her head began to clear, the disturbing faintness receded, and as it did she cursed herself for showing such weakness before this hard, unyielding man.

'I'm all right now,' she managed, determined to try to speak, though she could have wished that her voice was stronger and less uneven.

'Keep your head down for a while. You've had a bit of a shock.'

That, Ginny thought grimly, had to be the understatement of the year. The haziness had almost completely faded, but she still kept her head bent. Not in obedience to his instructions, she told herself rebelliously, but because she needed time to collect her thoughts, regain some degree of composure and assess just how she was going to handle the situation from now on.

'And you probably need something to eat. After all, it is nearly three o'clock.'

Three o'clock? Ginny's head came up at a foolhardy speed, reviving that sickening swimming sensation. Determinedly ignoring it, though her fingers clenched on the bedspread with the effort, she turned wide, startled eyes on the man before her.

'Three?' How long had she lain on that bed, out cold, oblivious to everything that was happening? And how far could they have travelled in six or so hours? 'Where *are* we?'

A smile crossed the man's lips, but it was a cold, cynically amused travesty of a smile, and one Ginny hated on sight.

'You really don't expect me to answer that, do you?'

She'd been wrong about the concern in his voice earlier. In her weakened state she must have imagined it, needing to hear it. There was no trace of any such emotion now; his voice was steely hard and his eyes seemed to have lost some of their glowing colour, so that they were just chips of pale blue ice.

'That information is strictly classified—but I will tell you that you're far enough away from Marshall to make it impossible for you to get back there without a car. So I suggest you resign yourself to staying here for a while.'

Resign herself? He'd picked the wrong woman if he thought she was simply going to sit back and let him get on with his cold-hearted scheme. She had little doubt that Gavin Marshall would be well able to pay whatever ransom he would demand, but it wasn't Marshall she was thinking of, it was Jamie and Lisa, and come hell or high water she was going to get them out of this mess if it was the last thing she did! But for now it was probably safer to pretend to go along with him. If he thought that she'd given in, then perhaps he might relax, grow careless, and when he did...

'I see.' She tried hard with her voice, and was pleased to find that it sounded every bit as resigned as he could have wanted. 'Well, at least I know where I stand.' The next bit was more difficult; she hated the thought of having to ask this man *anything*, and was afraid that the words would stick in her throat, but in the end her overriding concern made things easy. 'Could I see the children?'

'Of course.'

The ease with which he agreed disconcerted her. She had expected resistance, had determined to plead if that was what it took, though it made her feel sick to think of doing any such thing. His swift acquiesence rocked her so that she could only manage a murmured, 'Thank you.'

'But there are one or two conditions attached to that.'

Of course. There would be. The momentary sense of unreality faded, leaving her once more calmly in control of herself. At least she now knew just what sort of a man she was dealing with.

'What sort of conditions?'

'We'll come to them in a moment. First things first. We're likely to be together for a while, so perhaps I'd better introduce myself. My name's Hamilton—Ross Hamilton.'

Just how was she expected to respond to that? Ginny's grip on reality slipped again as she struggled with a hysterical desire to laugh. This couldn't be happening! She was being held prisoner in a house she didn't know—in heaven knew where—and her kidnapper was politely introducing himself for all the world as if they'd just met at some smart society function!

Her eyes went to Ross Hamilton's face. It was an intelligent face, she admitted, surprisingly so for a thug, a criminal. In any other circumstances those clear, bright eyes and wide forehead would have led her to think of the mind behind them, and she would have been surprised—and disappointed—if he hadn't proved to have a brain that could more than match her own. If they *had* met at a party or some social function, she could well have been drawn to him because he was the sort of man who would stand out in a crowd.

Her initial reaction to him, heightened by fear and stress, had created an image of an overpowering height and strength, but seen through calmer eyes he was nothing like as big as she remembered, though average was not a word she would apply to him. His muscled build and that glossy black hair prevented the use of any such term. He wasn't conventionally handsome, but there was something about that strongly carved face, those electric blue eyes deep-set under dark, straight brows, that would draw many women's gaze. It had a compelling, forceful attractiveness that was all male.

'And you're—Ginny.'

How had he known that? Ginny was unable to hide her surprise, but even as her eyes opened wide in astonishment she remembered. Jamie had called her name. He had got out of the car and had been coming towards her, just before——

'You hit me!' The indignant words tumbled out, catching Ginny herself as much by surprise as they evidently did Ross Hamilton.

'No—you fell against the car. It wouldn't have happened if you hadn't panicked. There was no need for that. I only wanted the children. I would have let you go unharmed, but you were so damn stubborn.'

Ginny barely heard his last words. *I would have let you go unharmed.* The quiet statement echoed over and over in her head. So why had he brought her with him, after all? It would have been much easier to have left her where she had fallen, so that he only had the two children to cope with. Would that have been better or worse? She shivered faintly, trying to imagine how she would have felt, coming round on that isolated road to find herself alone, with her car empty and the children gone.

Her *car*! Realisation hit home forcefully. He would have had to leave her car behind. Surely someone would have found it by now. And at work, Carol, her secretary, would have missed her, would probably have phoned her home to see if she was ill, and, not getting an answer—— It was a struggle to school her face into an expression that revealed nothing of the hope that flared suddenly in her heart.

'Why did you bring me here, then?' she asked hastily, using the question to cover the betraying hesitation.

Blue eyes locked with brown, his slightly narrowed as if the answer to her question wasn't easy to find.

'I've been asking myself that, too,' Ross replied on a note of irony. 'It would have been a hell of a lot easier to have dumped you in your car and left you there.'

His gaze moved away from her eyes, sliding down over her face and coming to rest on the dark, discoloured skin on the side of her jaw, a frown drawing his dark brows together.

'Does that hurt very much?'

Ginny blinked in confusion at the unexpected huskiness of his tone.

'It's sore,' she managed unevenly. 'What did you expect?'

Her voice faded as, very slowly, Ross reached out a hand towards the ugly bruise. His touch was delicate, surprisingly so for such a big man, and Ginny's flinch was more a matter of instinct than because she felt any real pain. But then, as the strong fingers lightly traced the shape of the injury, she was stunned to find herself suddenly a prey to a new and infinitely more disturbing set of feelings.

The cool brush of Ross's fingertips was soothing to her hurt flesh, stilling the uneasy thudding of her heart, so that her breathing became deeper, more relaxed. Though no words had been spoken, she felt as if there had been some communication of the deepest, most intuitive kind between them, and she struggled against an almost overwhelming desire to let her cheek rest against the palm of his hand. His eyes seemed to have darkened until they were almost completely black, his gaze holding hers for a long, silent moment. If she turned her head ever so slightly——

But then Ross took his hand away with an abrupt movement, and immediately she was jarred back to reality, forcing herself to remember that he was a cold, callous man who had kidnapped her and the children and was holding them captive for selfish, greedy reasons of his own. Her stomach lurched queasily as common sense gave her one very good reason why he hadn't left her behind on the road to Holme Hall. She had seen him up close, could give a good description of him and his car, possibly even its registration number—not that she could recall that at the moment, but Ross wasn't to know that. She was a danger to him—a threat. At once all her muscles tightened with fear and tension, her feelings made so much worse by the bewildering sense of loss that flooded through her.

'I'm sorry that had to happen——'

'You said I could see the children——' Their voices clashed as Ginny forced the words out, struggling to ignore the conflicting feelings that assailed her. She was alone and, she admitted honestly, terribly afraid. But was she so desperate for comfort that she would turn to this hard, unfeeling man for it?

Ross nodded silently. He appeared abstracted, his mind on something else.

'But there were—conditions,' Ginny prompted unevenly.

'Yes.'

For a moment longer those strangely thoughtful blue eyes lingered on her face, then abruptly his mood changed, that coldly indifferent look snapping back into place, and he was once more the hard, determined man, completely back in control.

'If I let you out of this room I have to have your word that you won't try anything stupid. As I said, we're miles away from Epton—from anywhere, in fact. This house is completely isolated, so screaming or shouting for help won't do you any good at all. There's no phone installed, so you can't call the police, and I suggest you don't try any stupid escape attempts. Such actions would only frighten the children, and it's best for them if things can be as normal as possible.'

'Normal?'

Ginny couldn't help herself, the word escaped involuntarily. She might have said more, but a sudden flash of anger in those clear blue eyes silenced her, and she

quailed inside at the threat implied by the furious glare
he turned on her.

'I don't want those kids upset in any way!'

No, that wouldn't suit him at all, she could see that.
He would have no sympathy, no patience with a tearful
four-year-old or a terrified six-year-old. So how would
he have coped if she hadn't been here? Was that why he
had taken her along with them? Or—her blood ran cold
at the thought—had his spying out the land included an
investigation into her own background—her father's
highly profitable business?

'Do I have your word on that?' The sharp demand
broke into her disturbing train of thought.

Ginny's chin came up determinedly. Of course it would
be a lot easier—not to mention safer—to agree, give her
word without any further argument, but it galled her to
give in to this creature's demands so quickly. *She* was
no frightened child, and she was going to make damn
sure he realised that.

'I'm promising nothing.'

The look that crossed Ross Hamilton's face threatened
her conviction that she wasn't going to let him frighten
her into submission but, drawing on all her remaining
reserves of strength, she met those steely eyes with a defiance that she hoped was convincing, hiding the rapid
beating of her heart that was the result of the way her
stomach was twisting itself into tight, painful knots.

'In that case, you'll stay here until you do.'

His absolute calm was more shocking than if he had
lost the temper she had earlier sensed was only just in
control. He meant what he said, she knew, the set of
his jaw and the way his mouth was drawn into a firm,
resolute line told her that without any doubt.

'I'll bring you up something to eat.'

In the few seconds it took him to cross the room to the door, Ginny had time for a hasty rethink. If there had been only herself to consider, then he could make demands until hell froze over and she'd never agree to one of them. But there wasn't just herself—somewhere in this house were Jamie and Lisa, alone, not knowing what was happening to them. And if she was frightened, how must they be feeling? The children had to be her first concern, and that meant that no matter how much it went against the grain, she had to make at least some show of going along with what Ross Hamilton wanted.

'All right.' The words came out hoarsely, common sense and anxiety about the children warring with her own instinctive reluctance to give in. 'I promise I won't do anything that will upset or frighten Jamie and Lisa.'

That was as much as she could manage. There was no way she could promise not to try to escape or summon help in whatever way she could. But it seemed it was enough to satisfy Ross, and he paused in the doorway, turning back to her.

'Then you can come downstairs. But I warn you, one false move and you'll back up here before you know what's hit you—and I won't be so generous a second time.'

She could well believe that. Ginny was well aware of how close she had come to forfeiting any contact with the children by her defiance. She was going to have to watch her step very closely if she wasn't to risk him carrying out his threat and locking her up in this room where she could be no help at all to Jamie and Lisa.

With her head held stiffly erect, she marched towards Ross where he held the door open. As soon as she was close enough, he reached out and curled his fingers around the upper part of her arm, holding her in a way that, while it wasn't as painful as the bruising grip he had used on her earlier, was quite firm enough to control her, prevent her moving away.

'There's no need for that,' she muttered rebelliously, fighting an overwhelming urge to struggle, hating the touch of his fingers.

'Just making sure,' was the soft reply, but that mildness was belied by the ruthless determination she could see in his face, the compression of his mouth, the darkness of his eyes communicating an unspoken warning that Ginny decided she would be far safer to heed as she submitted unwillingly to his imprisoning grasp.

She wasn't about to make any rash moves, anyway, she told herself. She knew too little about this house they were in for a start, and there were so many questions she needed an answer to before she could make any plans. Where *were* they? And what had Ross done with his car? Was it in a garage or simply parked outside? If she could only get hold of the keys——

She'd stay quiet for now, pretend to go along with what Ross wanted because she had no alternative, but once she learned the lie of the land she'd watch and take note, and when she'd found out just how things were, *then* she'd make her move.

At least the distaste she'd felt when Ross had taken hold of her arm was a more normal reaction than earlier, when he had touched her face. Ginny felt queasy at the thought that she had actually *enjoyed* having his fingers caress her cheek. She couldn't imagine what had possessed her. It had to have been the after-effects of shock—or her brain had been muddled by the blow to her head.

The first surprise when she walked out on to the landing was the discovery that both it and the stairs were completely uncarpeted, bare wooden boards creaking beneath their feet. This would make things difficult. If it came to creeping out of her room in the middle of the night, it would need a great deal of care not to tread on some loose floorboard and give herself away.

'It looks as if you've just moved in—or are you on your way out?' she said, using the attempt at light conversation to hide the way her eyes were moving everywhere, noting the doors that opened off the landing, the long stretch of the stairs and hall leading to the front door, beyond which lay freedom.

There was no response from the man at her side. So we're playing it strong and silent, are we? she commented wryly to herself. Well, that suited her; the less she and this man had to say to each other, the better. And his reticence was hardly surprising; he wouldn't want to give away anything that she could use when—if—she ever got out of here. Or was this house in fact not his own? Would a kidnapper be likely to use his own home as a hideout when it might later be traced by the police? More likely he had simply rented this place for a time, and as soon as the ransom was paid he'd be off, vanishing into thin air.

At the foot of the stairs, Ross led her into a large room opening off the hall. Ginny had barely time to notice the deep red and cream colour scheme, the comfortable-looking settee and chairs positioned round an open fire—the latter surprisingly sensibly protected by a large fire-guard—before she realised that the room was not empty. She blinked in astonishment at the sight of Jamie and Lisa happily settled at the big dining-table, Lisa busy with crayons and a colouring-book, Jamie working concentratedly on a jigsaw.

'Ginny!' Lisa was the first to notice her. 'Look what I'm doing! It's a picture of a fairy——'

The rest of the little girl's rush of words faded to an indistinct blur as Ginny struggled to adjust to this new development. She had anticipated two lonely, terrified creatures huddled together, in need of all the comfort she could provide—so the contented, peaceful scene before her rocked her sense of reality, making her wonder if she had in fact been asleep and dreamed everything, and was only now really waking up.

But a glance at the man at her side, his eyes alert and coldly watchful, his hand still resting firmly on her arm, dismissed that illusion as the dream, making the reality of her situation even more nightmarish after that one brief escape from it. In the back of her mind she heard again the sound that had floated up from downstairs in the moment Ross had opened the bedroom door. *Laughter*—a child's laughter. At the time it hadn't really registered, but now, seeing Jamie and Lisa so unexpectedly relaxed and at ease, she felt at least one of her worst fears seep from her.

Another swift survey of the room revealed an assortment of toys: a doll and a pram, a farmyard full of animals, and a castle complete with an army of toy soldiers. Unwillingly she had to clock up a point in Ross Hamilton's favour, as she acknowledged that his careful planning had also included the provision of things to keep the children occupied and so less worried and afraid than she had anticipated. Perhaps, after all, he would have coped well enough without her. She couldn't understand why the thought left her feeling disappointed and strangely redundant.

'Are you feeling better now?' It was Jamie who spoke, lifting his head from his jigsaw, one piece still in his hand. 'Do you often faint like that?'

Faint? With a struggle, Ginny caught back the hasty denial that had risen to her lips. So that was what Ross had said had happened—that she had fainted! Well, she supposed it could have looked like that. She'd had her back to the children, and they were unlikely to have seen the struggle that had led to her knocking herself out.

'No, I don't often *faint*.' She gave the word a deliberate satirical emphasis, keeping her eyes on Jamie, in spite of the fact that she longed to let her eyes slide to Ross in order to see his reaction. She had a grip on her indignation now, and accepted that it was better for Jamie and Lisa to believe the version of events Ross had given them; it would upset them too much to know the truth. 'And I'm feeling fine now—just a bit hungry. You two must be starving.'

'No, we're not,' Lisa put in. 'Uncle Ross made us lunch.'

Uncle Ross? This time, Ginny was unable to stop herself as she turned her eyes on Ross, her astonished gaze being met by a blank, unrevealing stare.

What trickery had Ross used to cajole the children into giving him that affectionate title? Clearly he had found some way of winning their trust in the time she had been unconscious. Bribery, probably, she thought cynically, remembering the collection of toys. Evidently Ross Hamilton had invested a fair amount in this enterprise. How much could Gavin Marshall afford to pay in ransom? Thousands? More? Well, Mr Hamilton wasn't going to see one penny of the profit he hoped to make from his nasty little scheme, not if she had anything to do with it.

Or was that 'Uncle' just a name? The question sprang into her mind with a belated recollection of Gavin Marshall's mention of his brother-in-law. Was *this* the infamous uncle who Gavin so distrusted? And, remembering how the children's father had spoken of him, did that make their situation any less precarious? What possible reason could this man have for kidnapping his own nephew and niece?

'I'd have made you something, too,' Ross's voice put in quietly, 'but each time I looked in on you, you were still out for the count. But you'll need something now—I don't want you going faint on me again.'

His lips quirked into a quick, mocking smile as he caught Ginny's involuntary angry grimace.

'What would you like? There's no cordon bleu on offer, I'm afraid.' She was treated to another of those disturbingly attractive lop-sided grins. 'Basic supplies are all I've got.'

'Oh, anything—a sandwich.'

Ginny's response was jerky and uneven. The realisation that he had looked in on her—not once but several times—while she lay unconscious was intensely worrying. She had been dead to the world, completely vulnerable, and this brute of a man had stood by the bed looking down on her. Her blood turned cold at the thought, and unconsciously her hands moved over her blouse and skirt, as if to reassure herself that she was still fully dressed.

At least he had left her that degree of dignity, she thought thankfully. In some of the accounts of kidnappings she had read, the abductors had removed their victim's clothes in order to assert their power over them. Glancing up, she caught Ross's eyes on her, the blue eyes darkened by a new and frightening intensity. Immediately from feeling shiveringly cold she was suddenly burning hot, as if she had a fever. She lifted a hand before her face, as if to break the contact of his eyes.

'Cheese, ham or chicken?' The question was so ordinary, so mundane, that, with her mind still full of other, more worrying thoughts, she couldn't understand it for a moment, and simply stared blankly. 'In your sandwich,' Ross added, impatience sharpening his tone.

'Oh, cheese...'

She had to get a grip on herself. Her thoughts were wandering here and there when she should be keeping her mind firmly on the matter in hand, watching and observing, waiting for her chance. A man who had planned a kidnapping with as much care as Ross Hamilton had wouldn't be easy to outwit. She was going to have to think fast if she was to get herself and the children out of here.

'One cheese sandwich coming up.'

Ross disappeared through a door at the far end of the room which presumably led to the kitchen. Watching him go, Ginny took a deep breath, counting to ten slowly, then, ignoring Lisa's request that she look at the picture of the fairy, she dashed into the hall, moving as quietly as possible over the uncovered boards. The clatter of plates in the kitchen covered a creak that came from an unwary move, and before she had had time to consider what her next move would be she was at the door.

Her fingers were on the handle; taking another deep breath, she tightened her grip.

'Going somewhere?' the mocking voice she had already come to hate questioned drily, making her spin round in shock.

Ross lounged in a nearby doorway, his long body indolently at ease, and as she stared at him he lifted one hand slowly. Ginny's heart sank to somewhere under the soles of her feet as she saw the keyring dangling from one strong finger.

'You really didn't think I'd forget something as basic as locking the door, did you?' he drawled lazily, the sardonic tone grating on Ginny's taut nerves. 'Credit me with a little intelligence please.'

'It was worth a try,' Ginny managed breathlessly. Her heart was beating frantically with the tension of the short journey across the hall, and the shock of Ross's sudden appearance and she eyed him uneasily as he slowly straightened up. What would happen to her now? Would he carry out his threat of taking her back to her room and locking her in?

'Well, for future reference, perhaps you ought to know that this door and the back one—and all the downstairs windows—are well and truly locked and will remain so. And the only keys to them are here——' He patted the pocket of his jeans into which he had slid the keyring. 'And I'll make sure they'll stay there all the time. Now, perhaps you'd like to come back into the living-room and have something to eat.'

'You're not——'

Ginny couldn't bring herself to finish the question. If she did end up back in the upstairs bedroom, she would have failed in her primary concern to care for the children. Silently she cursed herself for her rash action. She should have known that Ross would have made sure that all the doors were locked, and she had risked everything on that one unthinking impulse.

The look Ross gave her was shaded with a mocking tolerance that set irritation pricking like pins and needles over her skin.

'Everyone's entitled to one mistake,' he drawled smoothly, making Ginny grit her teeth against the angry retort she longed to flash back at him. His condescension implied that her pathetic attempt at escape had been so foolishly naïve that it wasn't worth bothering to take any action over it.

And in a way he was right, Ginny was forced to admit. She had rushed into things without any forethought, and by doing so had risked blowing their tenuous truce wide open which, if he decided to retaliate as he had threatened, would leave her without any contact with Jamie and Lisa at all.

'Why don't you go and sit down and I'll bring the food in to you.'

The suggestion was made with a careful courtesy that eroded Ginny's control even further. She was struggling with the impulse to lash out at him, verbally at least, to give vent to the volatile mixture of fear, apprehension and boiling anger that was bubbling just under the surface like lava in a volcano. One more word uttered in that sardonic, taunting tone would be enough to make her explode.

Luckily at that moment a young voice interrupted them.

'Ginny?' Lisa's small figure appeared in the hallway. 'Why did you run out like that?'

Catching the note of uncertainty in the little girl's voice, Ginny cursed herself even harder. She had achieved nothing by her rash action; instead she had done what she had most wanted to avoid—she had made the child worry about her situation.

She didn't see the look Ross shot in her direction, but she felt it like a crackle of electricity in the air, and she couldn't be unaware of the stiffening of his body, the sudden tension in every muscle of the man at her side. He hadn't said a word, but the threat implied by the way he held himself dried her throat, so that it was an effort to answer Lisa's question in anything like her normal voice.

'I—just came to see if Mr Hamilton needed any help,' she managed, her voice husky with the effort she was making to control it. It would never have convinced an adult, but she was thankful to see that Lisa's mind was clearly on something else.

'Why do you call him Mr Hamilton? He's Uncle Ross.'

'Not to me.' It was impossible to erase the touch of venom that sharpened her voice. 'To me he's Mr Hamilton.'

'But that's not very friendly.' Jamie had joined his sister now. 'And we're all to be friends. Uncle Ross said so.'

Ross Hamilton is no friend of mine! Ginny's breath hissed through clenched teeth as she shot a furious glare in Ross's direction, meeting such a coldly warning look from those steely blue eyes that she shuddered involuntarily.

'Try Ross,' he suggested, the apparent mildness of his tone belied by the promise of retribution that darkened his eyes, sending a sensation like the trickle of icy water creeping down Ginny's spine.

Was Ross Hamilton even his real name? Privately she doubted it. He was hardly likely to give her that sort of information when it could be used against him later. But Ross was still watching her, waiting for her to respond. Swallowing hard, she acknowledged that, at this moment, discretion was definitely the better part of valour.

'Ross it is, then,' she said, her mouth twisting in distaste as she spoke the name, and found herself unable to resist adding, '*If* that's your name, then I'd better use it.'

Her tiny stab had no effect on Ross's composure. Looking straight into his eyes, she saw nothing beyond a touch of satisfaction at the way she had conceded the point about his name.

Well, enjoy your triumph while it lasts, Mr Hamilton, she told him silently, allowing herself to feel the defiance she didn't dare express openly. Let him think he had her cowed; she wasn't beaten yet, not by a long way!

But the next moment her composure was severely threatened as, with a small, puzzled frown that revealed the way he found adult behaviour totally incomprehensible, Jamie put in, 'Of course that's his name. He's our Uncle Ross—Mummy's brother.'

Ginny knew her shock and consternation must show on her face, and she cursed her own transparency as the mocking smile that curved Ross's lips revealed only too clearly that he was well aware of the way she was feeling.

So Ross *was* the uncle Gavin Marshall so disliked, the man he had been adamant he would never let come near his children. After her earlier fears, that fact should have come as something of a relief, but, with Gavin's description of his brother-in-law as the man who had tried to break up his marriage and who was an inveterate womaniser echoing inside her head, she felt a frisson of a new and more intensely personal fear at the realisation that the fact that she now knew who Ross was changed nothing. She was still trapped here, in this isolated house, with two small, vulnerable children, and she had no idea why Ross had kidnapped them or just what he had in mind for them now that they were his prisoners.

CHAPTER THREE

'ARE we going home soon?'

Lisa's question fell into a moment of silence, startling
Ginny so that she glanced up swiftly from where she was
helping Jamie with his jigsaw. For a terrible moment her
mind went completely blank, and she could think of no
way to answer the little girl.

What had remained of the afternoon had dragged
painfully slowly. With the disturbingly dark, watchful
figure of Ross a constant, worrying presence, Ginny had
had no chance to investigate the house any further. A
couple of trips upstairs on the pretext of going to the
bathroom had been all she could manage, and these had
revealed nothing beyond the fact that of the four bedrooms that opened off the landing only two were furnished, the one in which she had woken earlier and
another which, as it contained two single beds, was
clearly intended for the children's use.

But, well aware of the dangers of rousing her captor's
suspicions, she hadn't dared to linger any longer and
had hurried back down to the living-room where she had
concentrated on keeping the children occupied in the
hope that they would remain calm and unworried. She
had managed to keep up a pretence of relaxed ease, even
forcing herself to eat the meal Ross had provided, though
she felt that the smallest mouthful would choke her if
she tried to swallow it. She needed to eat to keep her
strength up, and so she had forced the savoury stew
down, relieved to see that the traumatic events of the

day had not affected the children's appetites in any way. In fact, both Jamie and Lisa appeared amazingly relaxed. Probably they were too young to understand their situation, accepting Ross as the kindly uncle he appeared to be, unaware of the undercurrents that made Ginny so tense with apprehension.

What possible motive could Ross Hamilton have for his actions? Gavin Marshall had made it very clear that he and his brother-in-law detested each other, but could Ross really hate his sister's husband so much that he would cold-bloodedly kidnap his children in order to hurt him? That thought made her feel sick, the insight into Ross's character it revealed stretching her nerves so tight that she thought they might actually snap under the strain.

As the evening had drawn in Ross had pulled the curtains against the gathering dusk and, if she hadn't known otherwise, Ginny would have felt that the scene in the living-room would have looked cosy and comfortable, a secure haven from the darkness outside. But her mind was full of Gavin Marshall and the way he must be feeling as night closed in and his children had not returned home, her thoughts so disturbing that Lisa's question came as a shock, jolting her out of her dark reverie.

In the end it was Ross who broke the awkward silence, his voice coming quietly from the shadowy corner where he sat.

'No, Lisa, you're not going home tonight at all. You and Jamie are staying here for a few days.'

His tone was pitched at just the right level, Ginny admitted unwillingly. It was gentle enough to make the statement sound like an invitation, but with just a touch of firmness that would squash any protest before it had time to form. At her side she sensed Jamie lift his head.

'We're staying here?' he asked, and Ginny was unable to interpret his tone. There was no trace of fear in it; in fact, if it hadn't been so unlikely, she would almost have said that the little boy sounded relieved.

'That's right,' Ross confirmed. 'It's a sort of surprise holiday—just you, Lisa and me.'

'And Ginny,' Lisa put in. 'Is Ginny staying, too?'

Ginny knew a desperate longing to be invisible as Ross's eyes went straight to her face, coldly amused and with that mocking gleam she detested in their blue depths.

'Oh, yes,' he said, his tone challenging her to protest, 'Ginny's definitely staying.'

'Where will we sleep?' Lisa's curiosity had been aroused.

'There's a room all ready for you upstairs. In fact,' he glanced at his watch, and the rush of relief at having that hateful gaze no longer directed at her face made Ginny aware of how tautly every muscle in her body had been held from the moment Lisa had first spoken, 'it's about time you were off to bed now, so let's have these toys packed away——'

To Ginny's astonishment, Jamie and Lisa began to obey him without a word and, to her even greater amazement, Ross himself got down on his hands and knees beside Lisa and helped her pack away the Lego bricks that were scattered across the carpet.

Watching the two dark heads so close together, Ginny was torn between a longing to snatch Lisa away, hating the thought of her even being close to this man, and a reluctant admission that Ross's behaviour was that of someone who liked and understood children, not at all that of a cold-blooded villain who had snatched Lisa and Jamie away from their father in order to use them as a weapon in whatever private war he was waging with Gavin Marshall. He couldn't be more unlike gentle, kind Sam, her own brother-in-law.

At the thought of Sam, a sudden shaft of distress and apprehension shot through Ginny, so that she almost gasped out loud. Her family, her mother and father, seemed so very far away. She didn't know the distance in actual miles, not having the faintest idea where she was, but emotionally she felt as if the whole world lay between them.

Had her car been found and traced back to her address, or had Carol tried to contact her and, not finding her at home, phoned her parents? All colour fled from Ginny's cheeks as she pictured her mother's reaction if she had been told that her daughter had disappeared—and how much worse must Gavin Marshall be feeling when *his* daughter was so very much younger. He must be frantic, distraught, imagining the very worst.

Oh, *damn* you, Ross Hamilton! Unable to keep still a moment longer, Ginny got to her feet, her abrupt movement drawing Ross's eyes to her at once. She knew he had noticed her loss of colour by the way his eyes narrowed assessingly, and the swift, dark frown that crossed his face was distinctly ominous, sending her thoughts along other, equally worrying paths.

What did he want from her? She wasn't involved in his vendetta against Gavin, so had he just decided that her presence here would help to keep the children calm and relaxed, or—a sour taste filled her mouth—had he heard of her father's money? She started violently as Ross spoke.

'I think it's time we got this pair into bed. Why don't you take Lisa up and give her a bath?'

Ginny wanted to dig in her heels, refuse to do anything he said, but just then Lisa's small hand slid into hers and, looking down into the child's upturned face, she realised that the little girl was almost asleep on her feet—and no wonder. The traumas of the day had been enough to exhaust a fully grown adult, let alone a child of four.

'Will you tell me a bedtime story, Ginny?' Lisa asked, and with a sigh Ginny acknowledged that nothing could be gained by defying Ross any further. Whatever the cost to her own composure and self-esteem, the children were her primary concern, and she had to go along with him for now, no matter how it galled her to do so. But later, when Jamie and Lisa were in bed . . .

'Of course I will.'

She was relieved to find that her voice sounded as steady and relaxed as she could have wished, though she couldn't control her thoughts and knew that her anger and hostility must burn in her eyes for Ross to see clearly. If he did, he remained completely unmoved, meeting her furious glare with a blandly indifferent expression that made her grit her teeth against the angry words she longed to fling at him. Her fingers tightened around Lisa's.

'We'll go up, then. Come on, Jamie.'

'But I just want to finish this!'

'*I'll* bring Jamie in a minute,' Ross put in, his tone quiet enough, but Ginny knew he could read her thoughts; he had understood her reluctance to leave the little boy alone with him and that had angered him, it showed in the coldness of his blue eyes, ominously threatening.

'I think it would be better if——'

'I said, I'll bring him.'

There was no mistaking the warning in his voice now, and as brown eyes clashed with blue over Lisa's dark head Ginny knew a frisson of fear, mixed with an intoxicating sense of triumph at having penetrated his armour of cool composure in this tiny way, at least. But common sense told her she would be a fool to take the matter any further. To do so would be to risk the sort of scene she had determined to avoid. Nevertheless, she couldn't resist another dig at him, however petty.

'And what am I supposed to do about nightclothes for the children?'

Disappointingly, it didn't throw him for a second.

'There are pyjamas and a nightdress in one of the dressing-table drawers in the bedroom. They should fit, I—took advice about the sizes.'

He would! Ginny fumed as she mounted the stairs. Ross Hamilton had this whole thing planned like a military operation, so what chance did she have of outwitting him? Not very much, she admitted more soberly, ruefully acknowledging the lack of success of her attempts so far. Ross had checkmated every move she had tried to make.

Tired as she was, Lisa just managed to stay awake during the story Ginny told her, but by the time the last words had been spoken and she had been tucked in and given a goodnight kiss she was already drifting to sleep. Jamie, however, was a very different matter. Probably because he was older and so hadn't accepted the story of the 'holiday' as unquestioningly as his little sister, he seemed tense and restless, unable to settle after his bath, even though Ginny tried her best with a story that had held her two nephews enthralled on her last visit to her sister's house. Or perhaps, like Ginny herself, he was disturbed by the presense of Ross, who had brought the boy upstairs as Ginny was drying Lisa after her bath, and had remained, a darkly silent observer, setting Ginny's nerves jangling so that it was all she could do to concentrate on the story she was telling.

What did he expect? she wondered with a silent curse in the direction of his powerful figure, shadowed by the dim light of the bedside-lamp. That she would snatch up both children and leap from one of the windows with them in her arms? Oh, if only she could! But clearly she wasn't going to get any chance to try any such thing, not with Ross dogging her every move like some persistent, threatening bloodhound who refused to be put off the trail. Or perhaps he thought that she would tell the children the truth—or, at least, enough of it to expose the story of the 'surprise holiday' and kindly Uncle Ross as the fiction it was.

Well, he need have no worries on that score. If the story he had created kept the children from panicking, stopped them from crying themselves to sleep, wanting their father, then she wasn't going to blast it wide open, much as she would love to pull that particular rug from under his feet. And she had to admit that, so far at least, Ross's policy seemed to have worked. Neither Jamie nor Lisa had questioned why they were here and, more surprisingly, neither of them had even mentioned Gavin Marshall. Ginny's thoughts went back to her suspicion that perhaps the children's parents had been separated before Mrs Marshall had died. If that was the case, then perhaps they didn't know their father very well—and who was to blame for that? she thought on a flare of anger. Ross Hamilton, who had poisoned his sister's mind against her husband.

'Settle down, Jamie,' she said as the boy shifted restlessly once more. 'You've had a long day and it's time to go to sleep now.'

'I'm not tired.' Jamie was determined not to give in, in spite of the way the heaviness of his eyes revealed the truth about how he was feeling.

'Oh, yes, you are.' It was Ross who spoke, moving at last from his position by the door. 'As Ginny said, you've had a long day.'

Ginny scowled ferociously, hating the sound of her name on this man's lips, and she got to her feet hastily as he came to sit on the bed, not wanting to be forced into such unwelcome closeness. The move meant that she missed Jamie's next, low-voiced comment, but she heard Ross's reply and her temper threatened to boil over once and for all.

'There's nothing to worry about, Jamie. Everything's fine.'

'Nothing to worry about?'

The words slipped out before Ginny had time to think if they were wise, and she regretted them immediately as she saw Ross's head swing round towards her. The shadows in the room made it impossible to see his face, but she didn't need to read his expression to know what was in his mind: the tautness of the powerful muscles in his back and shoulders spoke volumes for the fury he was fighting to keep in check, drying her mouth and setting her heart racing uncomfortably, none of her tension easing, not even when Ross turned back to Jamie.

'Off to sleep now, young man.'

Ginny had to admit to unwilling admiration for the way Ross kept the anger he was feeling from showing in his voice, which was calm and soothing enough to have inspired confidence even in her if she hadn't known better.

'Everything will be all right—and I promise I'll still be here in the morning.'

Disgust rose like bile in Ginny's throat, threatening to choke her if she had to stay in the room a moment longer, and she turned on her heel and marched out of the bedroom, pausing on the uncarpeted landing to try to regain some composure. Her hands clenched into tight fists at her side as she struggled against the desire to run back into the room and launch herself at Ross, to wipe that falsely reassuring smile from his face, her mind filling with glorious but impossible images of finding some heavy object and hitting him over the head with it, leaving him lying unconscious as he had left her, and making her escape. But that was impossible, and she knew it. For one thing, Ross was so very much stronger, and for another, she knew she could never do it, not even in these desperate circumstances.

She had only a few precious minutes to herself. Sooner than she had anticipated, and well before she was emotionally ready, Ross appeared at her side, grasping both her arms in a bruising grip as he shook her roughly.

'Just what the hell was all that about?' he demanded in a savage undertone, carefully pitched so that it wouldn't reach Jamie's ears through the half-closed door. 'What do you think you're playing at, risking upsetting the boy like that?'

'Me—upset him?' Ginny didn't have Ross's enviable control over her voice, and it came out high-pitched and sharp, revealing only too clearly her inner feelings. 'You've no room to talk, Mr Lord Almighty Hamilton! What do you think *you're* doing to Jamie—and Lisa? ''Nothing to worry about'',' she mimicked his words bitterly. '"Everything will be all right." Nothing to worry about? There's *you* to worry about, isn't there? You and whatever nasty little scheme you've got up your sleeve. That's enough to worry anyone!'

'Ginny—' The low-toned voice held a strong note of warning, but Ginny was beyond heeding it.

'Don't you "Ginny" me!' she snapped, making an attempt to snatch her arms away from his grasp and wincing as he simply tightened his grip, holding her easily so that unless she started a fight there was no way she could break free. '*Uncle Ross*!' She turned the affectionate name into a scathing insult. '"I promise I'll still be here in the morning" —too bloody right you will! And there's the only thing Jamie should be worrying about! Instead, you're playing on his feelings, making him feel safe, getting him to trust you—and it's all just a damn lie!'

'Would you rather I terrified the life out of him?' Ross retorted coldly.

'At least that would be some sort of honesty—not like this blatant manipulation of a child's feelings! You make me sick!'

She tried another half-hearted attempt to free herself, and this time, to her surprise, Ross released her swiftly, taking a step backwards and letting his hands fall to his sides. Ginny couldn't interpret the look in his eyes, all she knew was that the gleam that lit them suddenly wasn't one of anger but something else. Could it possibly be admiration? Immediately she dismissed the thought as foolish, wishing Ross would look away. That intent, dark-eyed gaze was infinitely disturbing.

'I think we'd better talk,' he said quietly. 'Why don't you come downstairs?'

'I'm going nowhere with you! I've had all I can take from you for one day. I'm tired and I want to go to bed.'

This last was true. Now that Ross had stopped fighting her, she was suddenly overwhelmed with exhaustion, and her whole body sagged as if the tension between them had been all that had been keeping her upright. The bruise on her jaw ached horribly, and she was well aware of the fact that the after-effects of the fall and the tiredness she was feeling prevented her from thinking clearly. What she needed was a good night's rest, and maybe in the morning—As she thought longingly of the oblivion of sleep, another thought struck her, making her swing round to Ross again.

'Where am I going to sleep tonight?' There were only two bedrooms furnished. Ross had been well-prepared for the two children, but he obviously hadn't planned on her presence at all.

'You can have the bedroom— I'll make do with the settee downstairs.'

If he expected thanks for his consideration, he could think again, Ginny reflected satirically, then was suddenly thrown back into confusion as Ross's expression changed to one that, in any other circumstances, she might almost have believed was regret.

'I'll have to lock you in again. I can't risk you making any foolish moves.'

She'd expected that, but the thought of being imprisoned still sent prickles of panic shivering over her skin.

'But what if one of the children wakes up and calls out?'

'They won't.' Ross's confidence grated on her raw nerves. 'But if they do, I'll hear them.'

Much good you'll be! Ginny was tempted to retort, but then, recalling how Ross had handled Jamie's reluctance to sleep, she bit the words back with an effort. Honesty forced her to admit that Jamie had accepted Ross's reassurance more readily than her own. She strongly suspected that the little boy was rapidly developing a dose of hero-worship towards his uncle, which could complicate matters terribly, laying him open to a devastating disillusionment when Ross was finally revealed in his true colours, as he inevitably must be— which made it all the more imperative that she got both children out of here as soon as possible. But not tonight; she couldn't think of anything else until she had had some sleep.

'You can do what you like,' she said flatly, too tired now even to try to fight him any further. 'I'm going to bed.'

She choked back an absurd impulse to add a polite 'goodnight'. Men like Ross Hamilton didn't merit even the most basic of courtesies.

As she crossed the landing she was intensely aware of Ross's eyes following her. She could almost feel their gaze resting on her, making her skin burn where it touched, and automatically she gathered together the last remaining shreds of her strength and with an effort straightened her shoulders, drawing herself up stiffly and holding her head proudly erect. She had no intention of letting him see how close to collapse she was.

'Ginny——'

The softly spoken use of her name was positively the last straw. If only he knew how much she longed to hear a friendly voice speak her name with warmth and affection so that she wouldn't feel so despairingly, terrifyingly lost and alone. To her total consternation, hot tears sprang into her eyes and she blinked them back furiously, refusing to let them fall. She couldn't bear it if Ross was to see this final betraying sign of her weakness and know that, for tonight at least, he had won.

'Ginny——'

Driven beyond control, she swung round, brown eyes flashing fire.

'Why don't you go to hell?' she spat at him, then, knowing that she was capable of nothing more, and terrified of finally breaking down in front of him, she fled into the bedroom, kicking the door closed behind her.

The silence that followed was worrying. Having nerved herself for the sound of the key in the lock, Ginny couldn't imagine why Ross was taking so long about securing the door. Surely he couldn't be having second thoughts? She stood tensely in the middle of the room, knowing that she couldn't give in until she had heard him go downstairs, leaving her safe from disturbance at least until the morning.

The seconds lengthened into minutes, drawing her nerves so tight that she thought they might actually snap under the strain, and then, just as she was at screaming pitch, she heard the soft, grating sound of the key being inserted in the lock and the final, decisive click as it turned.

Although she had been expecting it, it sounded worse than she had imagined, bringing home to her the reality of her situation in a way nothing else had done before. She was a prisoner, locked in this room by that detestable, heartless man, a man who had callously involved herself and the children in his campaign of hate against his brother-in-law.

Wearily she dragged herself over to the bed and sank down on it. Her head ached, her jaw hurt abominably, and although she knew she should be using this brief time of quiet and privacy to try to think of some way of escape her mind refused to function. If she just closed her eyes for a moment...

Ginny never knew exactly what it was that woke her. Perhaps it was the strangeness of the bed or some unexpected noise from outside, most likely it was the need to free herself from a dream in which she was aware of nothing beyond a pair of icy blue eyes and a softly husky voice saying, 'Then I'm afraid you leave me with no alternative...' But one moment she was soundly asleep, the next she was sitting upright, wide-eyed and shaking, staring blankly round her in the dim light of the moon that shone through the uncurtained window.

At first, with her eyes still blurred by sleep, she didn't recognise the room, and for one wonderful moment thought the whole thing had been a dream, but then, as her vision cleared, the truth came rushing back and she groaned aloud.

'Oh damn, damn, damn you, Ross Hamilton!' she muttered, then paused, her eyes going to the clock on the bedside table.

The illuminated hands told her it was almost half-past one. Surely Ross would be asleep by now? Even kidnappers had to sleep some time! For a minute she listened hard, straining her ears to catch the smallest sound, but heard nothing. The still blackness of the room hung oppressively round her, but to Ginny the darkness and the silence were all she could have asked for. Her sleep had refreshed her—the pain in her jaw had receded to a dull ache and her mind no longer had that fuzzy, hazy feeling—and if Ross was asleep then she had been given a tiny, fragile thread of a chance—one she was determined to seize with both hands.

Very, very carefully she eased herself off the bed and on to the floor. Moving silently in her stockinged feet, she crept across the room to the window where with a silent prayer that, believing he would be sleeping in this room himself, and never suspecting that he would have a third captive to deal with, Ross might not have been quite so thorough in his precautions up here, she reached out and tried the window catch.

For a second it didn't move, and her breath caught in her throat as she tried again. Just as she was about to give up hope, the catch gave and the window swung outwards. Unable to believe her luck, Ginny simply stared for a moment, then, gathering her thoughts, she eased herself on to the window-ledge and peered out.

No, that was a mistake. The ground looked so very far away, her head swam and she clutched the wall desperately, her knuckles turning white with the pressure. She couldn't do it!

And did she really need to? Surely by now Gavin Marshall would have contacted the police? Knowing how his brother-in-law detested him, wouldn't he immediately suspect Ross's involvement in the children's disappearance? Wouldn't it be safer just to wait?

But Gavin had said he had no idea where Ross lived, and she couldn't forget the abhorrence with which he had spoken of the other man, his dread of Jamie and Lisa coming under Ross's influence—something which Jamie's reaction had shown to be an all too likely possibility. Did Ross plan to poison the children's minds against Gavin, as he had done with their mother? She couldn't let that happen. Drawing a deep breath, she forced herself to look again.

Luck was really with her. On the left-hand side of the window a thick, bushy ivy grew up the wall of the house. She could hold on to that and lower herself to the ground. The path below was only narrow, beyond that it was all lawn which should cushion her if she fell. No, she mustn't think of falling! If she was careful, she could do it.

It would mean leaving Jamie and Lisa behind. Their room was only feet away from her across the landing, but that locked door made the distance seem like a vast, unbridgeable chasm. But if her luck held she could find another house, telephone the police and be back again with help before Ross woke and came to her room to find her gone.

She was wasting precious time. Hastily Ginny collected her shoes and tossed them out the window, then, with her heart in her mouth, she eased herself on to the sill and twisted round carefully until she was standing with her back to the drop behind her.

Inch by careful inch she edged towards the bushy ivy, clinging on by her fingertips and toes. It was an effort to breathe normally: her mouth and throat were dry and her heart was thudding so hard that she had the irrational fear that the sound of it would be loud enough to wake Ross, who was sleeping in the living-room on the opposite side of the house.

Her fingers were cramped, her toes icy cold, but at last she reached the ivy and caught hold of some of the trailing creepers. Would it hold her weight? It would have to—she had come so far now, and she couldn't face going back. Summoning all her courage, she grasped the ivy and swung her weight over. For a long minute she hung there, her mind a blur of relief, then there was a terrifying creaking, cracking sound, and the next moment her tenuous support gave way and she fell, hurtling towards the ground.

CHAPTER FOUR

VISIONS of broken arms and legs, cracked ribs or worse, flashed through Ginny's mind. She felt her blouse catch on a jagged twig and heard it rip; then, just as she tensed in anticipation of the inevitable pain of landing, she found her fall cushioned by something firm and warm into which she crashed before being gently lowered to the ground.

For a few seconds the relief was so intense that it forced everything else from her thoughts, but then she heard a voice from somewhere above her, its hard tones only too familiar.

'You bloody crazy idiot! What the hell possessed you to try a trick like that?'

Perhaps, after all, landing on the ground would have been preferable, Ginny thought miserably. It might have hurt more, but at least she would still have had a chance of getting away. As it was, she had fallen, quite literally, straight into Ross's arms. A sickening wave of despair and disappointment swept over her.

'You should have known that ivy wouldn't hold your weight! What sort of idiotic escapade were you thinking of?'

'I should have thought that was quite obvious,' Ginny managed shakily.

Her head was beginning to clear, the shock of her fall slowly fading, though every muscle in her body ached, jarred by her abrupt landing. She couldn't meet Ross's eyes until she felt more composed, and she fixed her gaze on the dark blur of his feet, planted firmly on the soft grass just a short distance away from her.

'And it wasn't an *escapade*; I was trying to get away.'

To her complete consternation she heard Ross laugh, a sound so unexpected and so disturbingly warm and out of character with the cold-hearted kidnapper she knew that she glanced up swiftly, seeing the gleam of his eyes in the moonlight.

'Don't you ever stop arguing?' His tone was a blend of two parts amusement to one part exasperation. 'Look, we can't stay here all night. Can you stand?'

'I don't know. I can try.'

Ginny longed to be able to ignore the hand he held out to help her, but when she tried to get to her feet she found that her legs were as soft and weak as cotton wool and wouldn't support her. Even then she would have gone on struggling stubbornly, ignoring Ross's offer of assistance, but he gave a muttered exclamation and the next moment she was gathered into his arms and lifted off the ground.

'Put me down!' she protested vehemently. 'I can manage by myself.'

'It looked like it,' Ross retorted with dry humour. 'And be quiet—you'll wake Jamie and Lisa.'

The thought of the children was enough to force Ginny to keep a check on her tongue. She had failed them, making a mess of the precious opportunity to escape; she didn't want them to wake and see her, dirty and dishevelled, imprisoned in Ross's arms.

'Did I wake you?' she asked, her voice low.

'I wasn't asleep. I—had things on my mind—one of them being the distinct possibility that you would try something like this.'

So he had anticipated her move all along, anticipated it and been ready to forestall it as soon as she tried anything. And now his vigilance would be all the greater, so that she was unlikely ever to get another chance. Miserably, Ginny cursed herself for messing things up, her disappointment combining with the embarrassment she felt at being held in Ross's arms like this to make her position unbearable, so that she struggled to break free from his confining grasp.

'Keep still,' Ross reproved gently, his breath warm against her cheek. 'I don't want to drop you.' And suddenly, bewilderingly, Ginny's mood changed from one of furious despair and anger at herself to one of purely physical awareness.

Because of the darkness she couldn't see Ross—he was just a shadowy shape among the blackness of the night—but although her eyes wouldn't function it seemed as if every other sense had become heightened, so that she was hypersensitive to the warmth and strength of his arms around her, the muscled tautness of his chest against which her head rested, the scent of his body and the heavy, regular thud of his heart beneath her cheek. Something quivered deep inside her, and to her complete consternation she recognised it as a feeling of pleasure—sheer, sensual delight at being held like this—by this man!

What was happening to her? That fall must have shaken her more than she had realised. Her brain must be scrambled—it had to be shock, the after-effects of that terrifying moment when the ivy had given way. She couldn't be *enjoying* being in Ross's arms! Rationally, it was the last thing she wanted.

But rational was the last thing such feelings were, and the flickers of excitement that slid through her veins couldn't be suppressed even by the supremely logical argument that Ross was a callous, cold-hearted man who was prepared to use two innocent children as pawns in his feud with their father. Hot colour suffused Ginny's cheeks, so that she was intensely grateful for the dark blanket of the night that hid her reaction from Ross as he shouldered open the door and carried her into the house.

In the living-room he deposited her on the settee and stepped back, turning to switch on the light. Instinctively Ginny lifted her hands, ostensibly to shield her eyes from the sudden brightness, but also to hide the betraying colour of her cheeks.

'How do you feel now?' Ross asked.

'I'm fine,' Ginny managed, her voice muffled by her concealing hands.

But the truth was that she felt very far from fine. The shock of the unexpected feelings she had experienced in Ross's arms now combined with the aching of her bruised muscles to make her feel shaken and distressingly weak. Reaction to the abrupt end to her abortive attempt at escape had well and truly set in, and she was devastated to find that her eyes stung with unshed tears.

'How about something to drink? Tea? Coffee? Or would you prefer something stronger?'

'Tea would be fine.'

It was an effort to speak, but she had to say something so as not to draw Ross's attention to her. A warm drink might calm her—she didn't dare risk the effects of alcohol on top of what she was already feeling. Her whole body felt as if it had just experienced an electric shock, with a sensation like pins and needles bringing every nerve-end alive. And perhaps while Ross was making the tea she would have a chance to pull herself together, adjust to the change in his behaviour. Because after that one angry outburst he had not reacted at all as she had expected. Instead, he had shown concern for her predicament, had offered help. He had even carried her inside! Under her hands she closed her eyes, trying to drive away that particular memory.

'I'll just put the kettle on, and then we'd better see to your injuries.'

Injuries? Hastily Ginny lowered her hands. The sight that met her eyes made her gasp out loud. Her blouse was torn and mud-stained, her tights in ribbons, and her left leg was badly grazed, the shallow cuts oozing blood. When she examined her hands, she saw that they too were scraped and battered.

'I——' she began awkwardly, struggling to sit up, but Ross pushed her unceremoniously back against the cushions.

'I'll see to it,' he said firmly. 'For once, let's have no arguing.'

'But I'll have to take my tights off!' Ginny protested unthinkingly. She couldn't bear to have him touch her, not with those disturbing sensations still affecting her, leaving her feeling frighteningly vulnerable and sensitive, particularly not now when, as her head cleared, she recalled Gavin's condemnation of Ross as a shallow playboy who had a new woman every week.

Ross had turned towards the kitchen, but her words made him swing round abruptly and their eyes met in a long, silent moment that sent a shiver of awareness down Ginny's spine, lifting the tiny hairs at the back of her neck in an instinctive, intuitive recognition of feeling that needed no words to communicate it.

Dear heaven, he had felt it too! That moment of heightened sensitivity when she had been in his arms had somehow transmitted itself to him, irrevocably changing the way they saw each other, so that now there was no chance of ever going back to the way things had been before. It was there in the way she saw him as she looked at him directly for the first time since he had brought her back into the house. Even knowing what he was, even with Gavin's words echoing over and over in her head, even though she told herself she detested and despised him for the way he was using Jamie and Lisa, all she could see was a devastatingly attractive man, one whose presence in the room set her pulse throbbing at such a rate that she was sure he must hear the pounding of her heart, read her reaction in her heightened colour and unsteady breathing.

'So you will,' Ross said at last, the words coming slowly and huskily.

His eyes dropped from hers to survey her body as she lay on the settee, and although initially Ginny was grateful for the breaking of that intense contact, she felt her throat dry painfully as his gaze swept over her, lingering at the curve of her breasts and hips, before returning to her face. His eyes were darker than before, and with a touch of fire burning in their blue depths.

'In fact, I very much doubt that anything you've got on could be considered wearable in the future.'

'But I've nothing else!'

It was like being in a film in which everything was being played out in slow motion. She had heard his words and responded to them, but her mind wouldn't focus properly, couldn't think beyond the immediate moment. Her world seemed to have shrunk until it centred round a pair of blue, blue eyes and a firm, strong mouth—a mouth that she now saw wasn't hard at all; the bottom lip was fuller than she had realised, softer, more sensual.

It was the sort of mouth she would very much like to touch, to feel its softness under her fingertips, her own lips.

A sudden movement caught her eye, and with a shock she realised that she had actually lifted her hand as if to do just that. Hastily she converted the unthinking action into one of smoothing down her torn shirt, then immediately wished she hadn't as she saw Ross's eyes follow the disturbed movement.

'Have—have you a dressing-gown or something I could use?' she managed stumblingly, her tongue seeming to have tied itself in knots, so that it was a struggle to get the words out.

Ross gave himself a tiny shake, as if he was dragging his thoughts back from somewhere a long way away.

'I think I could provide that,' he muttered, and headed for the door, looking very much like a man who wanted to escape from a situation which had just got completely out of control.

Which was exactly how she was feeling, Ginny reflected dazedly. How had this happened to her? How could she have forgotten what sort of man Ross was? How could her own physical reactions have driven all thought of what she knew of him from her mind?

She loathed the type of man Gavin had described: men who thought so little of women that they used them simply as playthings to be picked up one moment and then discarded the next when their novelty wore off. And Ross had treated the children in just the same way, using them for his own selfish reasons without a care for their feelings. Was she going to let herself forget all this simply because of the appeal of a pair of electric blue eyes, a sensual mouth, and a lithe, firmly muscled body?

No! She had to get a grip on herself, think only of getting away. She had to fix her mind on that one thing and push all other thoughts away, or she would find herself in very deep water indeed.

'I've run you a bath.'

Ross's sudden appearance in the doorway startled Ginny so that she moved unthinkingly, jarring her bruised muscles, and had to catch her lower lip in her teeth to bite back the groan that almost escaped her.

'I thought that would be the easiest way to get those grazes clean, and it might stop you being quite so stiff in the morning.'

The blue eyes were blank, expressionless, but Ginny had the distinct feeling that Ross was carefully holding himself in check. Had he too decided that if he dealt with her injuries himself it would bring them into a dangerous, potentially explosive proximity which, like Ginny, he was anxious to avoid?

'I've left the dressing-gown in the bathroom. Do you need a hand to get upstairs?'

'No, thanks.'

Ginny's answer came gruffly, and she kept her head averted, concentrating on getting up off the settee without too much discomfort. If he helped her upstairs he would have to touch her again, and she couldn't cope with that now, not with every nerve in her body still alive to the sight and sound of him, her skin still re-membering the feel of his arms as he had carried her into the house.

Moving stiffly, she made her way towards the stairs, holding herself carefully so as to avoid touching him as she passed him in the doorway, and praying he would interpret her behaviour as a natural care for her injured muscles. To climb the stairs was an effort, and matters weren't helped by the way Ross lingered in the hall, watching her every move, until at last, unable to bear his scrutiny any longer, she halted and turned back to him.

'You don't have to worry! I'm not going to leap out of the window again as soon as your back is turned,' she declared tautly, and heard once again the disturbingly warm sound of his quiet laughter.

'I should damn well hope not. One dramatic rescue is quite enough for tonight. And you wouldn't be able to try, anyway. I took the precaution of locking the bedroom door while I was upstairs.'

She had needed that, Ginny reflected as she reached the bathroom and thankfully closed the door behind her, had needed a reminder of just what sort of man Ross was—and why she was here with him in the first place. He might have felt that electric spark of awareness that had so stunned her, but it had had no effect on his coldly calculating mind, and with the ruthless efficiency with which he had planned every move so far he had made sure that he had forestalled any further attempt at escape on her part. She would do well to remember that the next time her feelings threatened to get the better of her.

Locking the bathroom door, she turned to look at herself in the mirror, and from the first swift glance every other thought fled from her mind as she gasped aloud in shock and horror. She had known that she looked a mess, but she hadn't realised just how bad things were. One sleeve on her blouse had been almost ripped away at the seam, and every single button had been torn from its fastening, revealing the white, lacy cups of her slip and the full curves of her breasts above them.

Remembering how Ross had looked at her, fiery colour burned in Ginny's cheeks as, with brusque movements, she stripped off the offending blouse, discarding it with a grimace of distaste. The rest of her clothes followed swiftly, torn off her as if by doing so she could also remove the memory of those blue eyes darkening in sensual appreciation as they lingered on her body.

After the initial sting of the water on her lacerated skin, the warmth of the bath was soothing to her aching body, and slowly Ginny relaxed, letting her mind become a complete blank. Without the tension created by Ross's presence she felt exhausted, every muscle limp with fatigue. That had to be the explanation for her crazy reaction earlier, she told herself; she was worn to a frazzle, beyond thinking logically. When her mind threw back at her the image of her own face, seen in the mirror only moments before, her auburn curls falling in soft disarray around cheeks that had an unexpected glow, her brown eyes bright with something that looked worryingly like excitement, she refused to let herself think about it, though she trembled suddenly, making the water quiver around her. Her tiredness *had* to be the reason for her behaviour; she couldn't bear to think it could be anything else.

'Are you going to stay in there all night?'

The note of impatience in Ross's voice carried clearly even through the closed door, jarring Ginny out of the relaxed mood into which she had drifted, jolting her back to reality as tension gripped her once more.

'I'll be down in a minute,' she responded in a voice that her tight throat made hoarse and uneven.

Ross had moved so silently that she hadn't heard his footsteps on the stairs, and even with the thickness of the door between them she felt frighteningly vulnerable, intensely aware of her nakedness as she got hurriedly out of the bath and reached for a towel. What would he do if she didn't join him as quickly as he wanted? With a shudder she reflected that he was perfectly capable of breaking down the door and dragging her out of the bathroom, the thought making her rush through drying herself, her abrupt movements destroying the last shreds of the small reprieve of peace she had managed to find.

It took every ounce of courage she possessed to go back into the living-room and face Ross again. The white towelling robe he had left for her covered her adequately but, being Ross's, it was several sizes too large and the neckline gaped disturbingly revealingly. Ginny was painfully conscious of the fact that, underneath the robe, she was completely naked, having rinsed through her underwear and left it to dry on the towel rail. She would need it to be clean for tomorrow—though heaven alone knew what she would wear over it, her clothes were far too disreputable to even consider wearing them.

In her absence Ross had stoked up the fire, and it was now roaring welcomingly in the grate, a small table with a tray of tea things drawn up before it. It looked a delightfully cosy domestic scene, Ginny thought, despair making her breath catch in her throat at the thought of how very different the truth was from that illusion.

'Come and sit down.'

Ross's tone was abrupt, and Ginny felt a flash of relief at the way he didn't look at her but stared deep into the fire, his mind clearly on other things. But that relief was followed by a second, more disturbing feeling that she was shocked to realise was a stab of pique at the thought that, while she was so sensitive to him, he was apparently quite oblivious of her, that heightened awareness seeming to have vanished completely. Pulling the robe more tightly round her, she perched herself on the edge of the chair furthest away from him, her nerves too tightly strung to enable her to relax.

The cup of tea he silently handed her was welcome and she sipped the hot liquid gratefully, determined to make no effort to speak until Ross did. She had nothing to say to him, nothing that was in the least ladylike anyway, and she was damned if she was going to make polite conversation with this man!

Her resolve lasted the length of time it took to drain the first cup of tea, but as she lifted the teapot to refill it her companion's brooding silence became too oppressive for her to stand and, setting the pot down with a distinct thud, she rushed into unguarded speech.

'How long are you going to keep us here?'

For a moment she thought that he hadn't heard her, his attention concentrated on the fire, a dark frown creasing the space between his brows; but then, slowly, he turned his head and she saw his broad shoulders lift in an indifferent shrug.

'As long as it takes.'

'As long as what takes? What exactly do you hope to gain by this? Is it just a question of ransom, or what? Have you been in touch with Mr Marshall yet to let him know what's happened?'

She was disconcerted and disturbed by the way his eyes narrowed, as if something she had said had puzzled him, but the need to know exactly where she and the children stood cut through her momentary confusion.

'Well? *Have* you contacted him?'

'Not yet.' Ross's reply was as coolly unconcerned as his emotionless blue eyes.

'Why not? Isn't it bad enough that you've kidnapped his children without leaving him to suffer like this, not knowing what's happened to them? I can imagine what he must be going through—'

Her words died in her throat at the flash of something dangerous in those electric blue eyes.

'Can you?' Ross demanded aggressively. 'Can you really imagine how that feels? You don't know the half of it, lady! I'll contact Marshall when it suits me and not before—and until that time comes he can stew in his *feelings*!'

His mouth twisted as he emphasised the word with bitter cynicism. 'I wouldn't want to shorten the time he felt that way by one second.'

Disgust mixed with panic, threatening to choke Ginny as she saw the black, burning anger that turned Ross's face into a mask of savage anger. *This* was the real Ross Hamilton, the man Gavin Marshall had been so determined he would never let come near his children—and now she could see exactly why he felt that way.

At times during the afternoon, seeing the tolerant amusement with which Ross had regarded the children, the quiet, firm way he had handled them, she had found it hard to believe that he was capable of the hatred Gavin had described, but now at last he had revealed himself in his true colours, and they were every bit as loathsome, cruel and thoroughly despicable as Gavin had led her to believe. Just what had caused the breach between them? It was true that she hadn't taken to Gavin at their meeting, but he appeared to be a reasonable, concerned, caring father.

'What sort of animal are you? How can you be so indifferent to another person's suffering? I just don't believe anyone could be so totally callous—'

'*Suffering?*' Ross's hard, mirthless laugh shocked her into silence. 'Suffering?' he repeated sardonically. 'As I said, lady, you don't know the half of it.'

'Then tell me what all this is about. Not that I believe you could give me any explanation that would justify the way you've behaved, but if you could just tell me *why*——'

She broke off abruptly as Ross slammed his cup down on the table, shrinking back in her seat as he got to his feet to tower above her, dark and dangerous and terrifyingly threatening.

'Listen, lady, I don't have to explain anything to you! You're Gavin's——' He broke off abruptly, pushing one hand roughly through his thick dark hair, then went on more quietly, 'Look, this is between Marshall and me, and if you've any sense you'll keep out.'

'But I can't keep out!' Ginny scrambled to her feet, determined to cut down the advantage his height gave him, which made her feel far too vulnerable. 'I'm involved in this whether I like it or not. *You* involved me in it from the moment you brought me here!'

'So I did.' To Ginny's intense relief, the violence had faded from Ross's voice, leaving it dull and flat. 'Though lord knows why. You're a complication I'm not sure I can afford. It would have been much easier if I'd left you where you were.'

His eyes went to her face, dark and brooding, studying each feature with a strange intensity, almost as if he wanted to imprint every detail on his mind for ever.

'One hell of a lot easier,' he went on, as if to himself.

What was going through his mind? What had he planned to do that made her presence a complication he couldn't afford? 'You're Gavin's—' he had said. Gavin's what? His friend? Did he think she was more to Marshall than an employee; and, if so, would he think that to include her in his vindictive scheme would hurt his brother-in-law even more?

'And now that you've got me here?' In spite of her efforts, her voice shook revealingly, betraying the turmoil of her thoughts. 'What are you going to do with me?'

The look Ross turned on her was coldly assessing, making her think uneasily of a powerful predator that had cornered its prey. Her stomach lurched queasily. Why had she ever asked the question? Did she really want to know the answer to it? She had never felt so alone and vulnerable, trapped here with this man who had proved himself a cold, uncaring creature, one who regarded women as simply existing for his own pleasure.

'That rather depends on you. If you behave yourself you'll come to no harm—but any more clever tricks like tonight's little escapade...'

He left his sentence unfinished, but Ginny didn't need to hear the threat put into words. She could well imagine what sort of retribution Ross would mete out if she put his scheme at risk again. Her mouth felt dry with apprehension, and she had to swallow to relieve it.

'You can't expect me just to sit back and let you get away with this!'

Another of those steel-eyed glances flicked over her, sending a frisson of fear feathering down her spine and making her wonder how, even in the aftermath of shock, she could ever have thought this man remotely attractive.

'I expect you to see sense.' The silky drawl was belied by the icy hardness of his face, the promise of danger in his eyes. 'I've planned all this for a very long time, and I don't intend to see it fail just because of some fool of a woman who can't bear to be away from her creature comforts and her high society life for a few days.'

The scathing contempt in Ross's voice made Ginny wonder if, for the first time, she had some sort of a clue as to what motivated this man. If he had been watching her he would know about the agency, might have discovered how her father had provided the initial capital to set her up in the business. Although she would never actually describe her life-style as 'high society', there was no denying that she had never wanted for anything, and she was well aware of the fact that starting her own business would have been very much more difficult without her father's help.

Was this what Ross had against Gavin Marshall? Had some sort of inverted snobbery made him irrationally jealous or disapproving of anyone with money—something Gavin certainly had in abundance. This cottage, though it couldn't compare with Gavin's mansion, was comfortable enough, but did it actually belong to Ross— and had things always been that way?

'So you'd better get it into that pretty head of yours that nothing and nobody is going to stand in the way of my seeing this through. There are two ways we can play this—the easy way, where you face the fact that you're not going to get away and the best thing you can do is to learn to adjust to the situation. If you give me no trouble, I give you my word that you'll come to no harm.'

'And the—other way?' It was just a whisper, a thin thread of sound, but Ross caught it and the corners of his mouth curved into a smile that Ginny hated on sight.

'I don't have to go into details, do I? Just keep up this resistance, these stupid escape attempts, and you'll find out. But I sincerely hope you won't drive me to that——'

Suddenly, shockingly, his mood seemed to change. The cold, hard voice had softened, becoming bewilderingly gentle, and as Ginny stared at him, transfixed by the husky, caressing quality of his tone, he reached out a hand and trailed the backs of his fingers slowly down her cheek.

'There's no need for things to be like this,' Ross murmured seductively and, lost in the darkness of his eyes, Ginny unconsciously drew a long , sighing breath, her body leaning towards his as if drawn by some irresistible force.

Then in the back of her mind she heard Gavin Marshall's voice, and reality hit her like a dash of icy water in her face. The trance that had held her mesmerised snapped abruptly, and with a violent jerk of her head she repulsed Ross's caressing fingers, taking several hasty steps backwards, out of reach.

'Don't touch me! Keep your hands to yourself, you bastard! You may have the upper hand right now, and I'll have to do as you say because I've no other option— but *nothing* gives you the right to touch me! And if you try it again, I promise you that you'll regret it!'

With a small flare of triumph she saw that her attack had disconcerted him, at least momentarily. He let his hand fall to his side and stood watching her, those bright blue eyes intent on her face, as if trying to read whether she really meant what she said. So Gavin Marshall had been right—Ross Hamilton truly imagined that every woman he met would fall under his spell.

Well, she would convince him that she meant every word if it took all the strength she possessed, Ginny resolved, though the touch of his fingers had revived unwanted memories of those moments of sensual awareness she had felt in his arms, threatening to destroy her hard-won control; and the caress, light as it had been, had started a sensation like the fluttering of a thousand butterfly wings deep inside her.

'If that's what you want——'

'You're damn right it's what I want! Do you think I'd want *you* to touch me? I can't bear the thought of you even coming near me—it would contaminate me!'

Unconsciously she lifted a hand to rub at her cheek where his fingers had caressed it, as if trying to erase the imprint of his touch, but even as she did so she was forced to admit that the gesture was as much an expression of her own disgust at herself for not having struck his hand away immediately. She knew what this man was, Gavin Marshall had told her of all the other women, and yet, for a brief space of time, she had been weak enough to succumb to his skilfully seductive expertise. Her inner unease made her rub harder, trying to use the small, physical pain to counteract the disturbed feeling that assailed her.

Ross took a step towards her, just a single step, but it was enough to have her backing away, her brown eyes flashing defiance.

'Keep away! I said I don't want you near me.'

With half the room between them she paused, feeling just a little bit safer.

'In future, this is as close as I ever want to be to you.'

That hateful smile surfaced again, the light of mockery that gleamed in the blue depths of his eyes incensing her.

'My, we do over-react to one little touch, don't we? Isn't there a saying somewhere about a lady who protests too much? And as for keeping my distance, I'm afraid that will be just a little difficult, my beauty. Because, you see, I intend that you'll be sharing my bed for the rest of tonight.'

CHAPTER FIVE

'I'LL——' Ginny's mind threatened to blow a fuse. She forgot all about the dangers of her situation, her resolve to play along with Ross, keep him calm by appearing to do as he wanted. 'Like hell I will!' she spat at him furiously. 'I'd sooner sleep with the Devil himself than with you!'

Not that there was all that much difference, she told herself. Right now, Ross Hamilton seemed like the Devil incarnate. There was certainly very little to choose between him and Old Nick, and that smile was positively fiendish in its tormenting triumph.

'I'm afraid you don't have any choice.' Ross's tone was infuriatingly reasonable; it was as if he was trying to explain a very simple fact to a rather slow child. 'As you know, there is only one bed apart from the ones Jamie and Lisa are already sleeping in.'

'But you said you'd sleep on the settee.'

'I know I did—but that was before your Houdini act from the bedroom window. I'm not going to risk that happening again—and I'm certainly not letting you sleep down here unsupervised,' he added swiftly, clearly anticipating the alternative suggestion Ginny had been about to make. 'You're a liability, lady, and the only way I can make sure I know exactly what you're doing is to be right there with you—and I warn you I'm a very light sleeper.'

He paused, the blue eyes searching her face, obviously waiting for her to make some comment. But Ginny had

nothing to say. What *could* she say? She couldn't fault
his argument, but that didn't mean she was prepared to
go along with it—and yet, what choice did she have?

'So, it's now almost three o'clock,' Ross went on,
taking her silence for acquiescence, 'and I don't know
about you but I could certainly do with some sleep—so
I suggest we go upstairs.'

'No!'

It was no good. Rationally, she might have accepted
that Ross was right, that this was the only way things
could be arranged if he wanted to ensure she didn't try
to escape again, but emotionally there was no way she
could go along with what he suggested. Her head came
up defiantly, brown eyes flashing fire.

'I won't do it! If you want me in your bed——' she
almost choked on the words '—you'll damn well have
to carry me!'

'OK, if that's the way you want it.'

The mildness of Ross's tone caught Ginny unawares,
freezing her thoughts for a moment so that she was
totally unprepared for the sudden move he made, moving
close to her, his arm going round her waist before she
was swung up into his arms.

'Put me down!'

Desperation gripping her, Ginny struggled wildly,
kicking out at him with all her strength, her arms flailing
as she tried to free herself.

'Be quiet, damn you!' Ross muttered through clenched
teeth as, still holding her with one hand, he clamped the
other over her mouth, stilling her furious protests. 'You
asked for this, lady. You had your chance to go quietly,
and you didn't take it——'

Even in the grip of the panic that blurred her thoughts,
Ginny caught a new note, one she couldn't interpret,

that roughened Ross's attractive voice. He's hating this every bit as much as I am! she thought on a wave of disbelief.

No, that couldn't be true. The way he was prepared to use the children to get at their father showed that she couldn't expect to apply any sort of conventional morality to his actions; she had to have imagined it. As a test, she tried another attempt at freeing herself and felt the arms that imprisoned her tighten like steel bands until a gasp escaped her from under the hand that sealed her mouth.

'I'm warning you, lady——'

There was no hesitancy in his voice now, that inexplicable huskiness must have been just a delusion, a fantasy created out of her need to hear some sympathy, some note of feeling from someone—anyone.

'You can decide to come quietly—in which case things will be a lot more comfortable for both of us—or you can carry on fighting and take the consequences. Either way, you're coming upstairs with me—and it you let out one squeak that wakes those kids, I won't be answerable for my actions.'

At his words, all fight left Ginny in a rush. She had temporarily forgotten Jamie and Lisa, but now all she could think of was the way they would feel if they woke up and came out of their room to see Ross manhandling her in this way. They would be terrified and, much as she hated Ross, she had to admit that so far he had handled things so that neither of the children had been upset. On this point, at least, she and Ross Hamilton were in total agreement. So she forced herself to stay still and quiet in his arms, denying the outraged fury that swept through her as Ross carried her out of the room and up the stairs.

At least there was one comfort to be found in all this; that heightened sensual awareness she had experienced when Ross had carried her into the house no longer tormented her. All she wanted was to be free of those restraining arms, released from this unwelcome closeness—which just proved that those earlier feelings had been, as she had suspected all along, the effects of the shock of her fall.

So it was with a jarring sense of disbelief that, when Ross dumped her unceremoniously on the bed, she felt the sudden coldness of her body with the withdrawal of the warmth of his with a sense of loss and loneliness that left her feeling utterly bereft.

It was chilly in the bedroom, she rationalised, that was all. There was no heating up here and she was wearing nothing under the towelling robe. That realisation had hot colour rising to her face as she sat up abruptly, turning to Ross who, to her consternation, had already begun to unfasten the buttons on his shirt.

'I can't sleep here. I've—nothing to wear.'

His hands stilled on the buttons, Ross regarded her steadily, one eyebrow drifting upwards in an expression of lazy mockery.

'True,' he murmured, and immediately Ginny wished she hadn't spoken as she saw the way his eyes went to the neck of her robe. She was horrified to find that it had been tugged loose in the struggle downstairs and now it gaped widely, exposing the curves of her breasts, her skin rosy pink with embarrassment against the white towelling.

With a choking gasp she tugged the two sides together, holding them with hands on which the knuckles showed white with tension as she forced herself to look straight into those sapphire-blue eyes. She felt burning hot and then shiveringly cold as she saw the way they had darkened until they were almost black, just a tiny rim of blue showing at the edge of his pupils.

'I—' she began, but the sudden change in his face, amusement changing to a worrying dark frown, froze the words on her lips.

'You're not wearing a ring,' Ross said abruptly.

A ring? His words were so unexpected that for a moment her mind went completely blank, but then, as she saw Ross's eyes on her left hand, a thought slid into her head, bringing with it a rush of relief so intense that it made her feel slightly dizzy. She didn't know why Ross had imagined she would be wearing a ring, but right now she didn't care. All that concerned her was that here was a possible way out of the situation in which she found herself. Surely even the womaniser Ross was reputed to be would respect her commitment to another man, even if that commitment was totally imaginary. If she could convince him she was engaged to someone else, then hopefully that would be enough to make him keep his distance.

'That doesn't mean anything.' She tried hard with her voice, and was relieved to hear it come out firm and confident. 'My fiancé and I don't need such symbols to prove our love for each other—and we do love each other—very much.'

She would have said that it was impossible for his face to have hardened any further, but now it became so coldly distant it could have been carved from granite. He turned on his heel and strode across the room to pull open a drawer with a violent movement. When he turned back to her, he held a pair of navy blue pyjamas in his hands.

'Will these do?' His voice was rigidly controlled, his jaw tight with the effort of holding back something. 'They'll be a bit big but—'

'And what about you?' Ginny blurted out, unable to interpret his attitude, not knowing if her scheme had succeeded or failed.

That rigid control slipped, his firm mouth twitching at the corners as if he was trying to suppress a smile.

'Never wear the things. I only have these because they were a present from my mother, bless her. She thought that if I insisted on living in a half-renovated cottage I should have something to keep me warm at night.' All traces of restraint vanished, and that smile grew into a wickedly sensual and devastatingly disturbing grin. 'Other than some*one*, that is.'

'Your *mother*...' Ginny echoed dazedly, struggling to ignore the appeal of that smile. It sounded completely wrong—this cold, hard man talking about his mother with such evident warmth.

The grin faded swiftly, Ross's mouth taking on the bitter twist she had come to dread.

'Even bastards have mothers!' he bit out caustically.

'Of course, I didn't mean—'

Ginny couldn't string any coherent words together as she struggled to adjust to the swift succession of moods he had just revealed. She was forced to face the fact that she knew nothing about this man, other than what she had learned from Gavin Marshall—a man who, by his own admission, hated his brother-in-law as much as Ross detested him.

'*Why* are you doing this?'

Even though her question was a complete *non sequitur*, Ross clearly understood what she was trying to say.

'Jamie and Lisa? Don't tell me you don't know.'

'Oh, I know Gavin said—'

The mention of his brother-in-law had been a mistake, Ross's face darkening with a savage anger that turned Ginny's blood to ice in her veins.

'I don't want to hear anything Gavin said!' he exploded. 'I don't want to hear anything about that man ever again. Here——'

He tossed the blue pyjama jacket towards her.

'You can have this—it should cover all the vital parts—and to spare your blushes I'll wear the trousers. You can change in the bathroom.'

Ginny cursed the swift rush of colour that revealed her relief at the compromise he had offered, hating the vulnerability it revealed. Without a word she slid off the bed and, with the jacket in her hand, headed towards the door.

'And in answer to your question——' Ross's harsh voice stopped her dead in her tracks '—I'm doing this because my dear brother-in-law happens to be the man I most detest in the whole world.'

'But why——'

'Damn you, Ginny!' Ross's voice was rough and uneven. 'I've had enough of your questions for one night. I need some sleep, even if you don't. So go and get changed and be quick about it!'

She needed to sleep too, Ginny admitted in the privacy of the bathroom as she discarded the towelling robe and slipped on the cotton jacket. Her bruised body ached sickeningly, and her mind was fuzzy with exhaustion. She would need all her energy if she was going to cope with whatever tomorrow might bring—but how was she ever to do that if she had to sleep in the same bed as that hateful man?

Her mind went back over the confrontation in the bedroom. Ross had told her nothing more than Gavin had already said. There had to be some reason why he hated his sister's husband so much, but he had avoided telling her what it was. In fact, his attitude implied that he believed she already knew all there was to know. Did he think there was more between her and Gavin than simply the relationship of employer to employee? No, if he had planned this kidnapping so carefully, he must know that Gavin was planning to marry again.

Images of Ross's face floated in her mind, convulsed with hate when he spoke of Gavin, cold and hard as tempered steel—and that devastatingly sensual, appealing smile. Her body suddenly felt burning hot, as if she was in the grip of a raging fever. There was no way she could sleep with him beside her—but she had to rest. She had to concentrate on that first man, a man so eaten up with hatred that he would use anyone and anything in order to get his revenge, for whatever reasons. Only then could she push from her mind all thought of that other Ross, the one whose magnetic appeal left her far too vulnerable.

The light was out when she returned to the bedroom, but the moonlight streaming through the uncurtained window lit the room almost as brightly as if it were day. Ross was already in bed, leaning back against the pillows, his hands linked behind his dark head. The few minutes it took Ginny to cross the room seemed endless. She was supremely conscious of his eyes on her all the time, his gaze so intent that she could almost believe her skin would scorch where it rested. She was only too aware of the amount of slender leg and thigh revealed by the short pyjama jacket, the knowledge making her feel weak and shaken, so that it was a relief to sink down on the bed when she finally reached it.

'That looks a hell of a lot better on you than it would ever have done on me,' Ross remarked quietly, and hearing the softness of his voice, the note of sensual appreciation that warmed it, Ginny felt her nerves tighten in apprehension. *This* Ross was a far more potent threat to her personally than even the coldly angry man she had left only minutes before.

Now that she was actually on the bed, she found she couldn't make a move to get *into* it. She wished desperately that the room was darker so that she couldn't see the powerful lines of Ross's chest and shoulders, the firm muscles, narrow waist, and the soft blackness of his hair in sharp contrast to the immaculate white of the pillows that supported his head. It wasn't that she was unused to masculine company. She had had plenty of boyfriends and, being so keen on swimming, had often seen many of them wearing even less than the cotton trousers she knew Ross had on under the blankets. But those had been just friendships. She hadn't yet met the man who could make her want to take the relationship any further—and none had affected her in the way that this hateful, callous man did.

'Are you getting into bed, or do you intend to stay there all night?' Impatience and mockery blended in Ross's tone, sparking off a prickling irritation in Ginny's mind.

'I'll get in when I'm ready and not before!'

Her retort was greeted with a muttered, exasperated curse, and a moment later the bedclothes were pulled from under her with a rough movement that almost threw her off the bed.

'Get in!' Ross ordered, his tone making it only too plain that she would be foolish to resist further, pushing her into action so that she scrambled hastily and inelegantly into the bed, pulling the blankets close up around her—but not before she had caught a glimpse of the navy cotton that covered his legs—the other half of the garment that she was wearing.

Suddenly the intimacy implied by that sharing of the clothing overwhelmed her and, cheeks burning hot, she twisted on her side, turning away from him to bury her face in the pillows, closing her eyes determinedly, though she knew that sleep had never been further away. Her discomfort was increased as she felt laughter shake the strong body so very close to her own, and Ross's voice was uneven with lingering amusement when he spoke.

'Anyone would think you were a virgin who'd never had a man in her bed before. Relax, my lovely. You'll never sleep if you stay as strung up as that.'

Relax? It took every ounce of control that Ginny possessed to resist the impulse to round on him, lashing out to wipe the smile she could hear in his voice from his arrogant face. But then the rest of his words sank in and her hands clenched into tight fists at her sides. Did he judge everyone by his own amoral set of rules, assuming that just because she was over twenty and unmarried she must have had dozens of lovers?

How many women had *he* slept with? Plenty, it seemed; certainly his lack of embarrassment at having a complete stranger share his bed seemed to confirm Gavin's accusations. What had those other women been like? Had they too felt the power of his arms around them, but in a very different way—their strength used to give pleasure, not to restrain? Had they known his kisses, the touch of his hands...

Dear lord, what *was* she doing? Had she really been imagining Ross as her lover? A movement on the other side of the bed told her that Ross was settling down to sleep, and Ginny held herself rigidly, desperately trying to avoid any contact with his hard body. But, try as she might, she couldn't prevent the warmth that emanated from him from seeping into her own body, easing some of the tension from her muscles, making her relax in spite of herself. In any other circumstances it would have been a feeling she could have enjoyed, a soothing, comforting sensation after the stresses of the day. Her body felt as if she had just done ten rounds with Big Daddy in the wrestling ring, and she longed for the oblivion of sleep.

But the initial sense of relaxation was very soon replaced by a new and very different feeling. A tingling sense of awareness flickered along her veins and she knew an intense longing to nestle closer to Ross, feel the muscular length of his body against her own. In her head she heard a pounding like the sound of distant thunder, and with a shock of disbelief recognised it as the throbbing of her own pulse. Restlessly she tossed and turned, but the movement only made things worse when her arms and legs brushed against Ross's warm strength, the tiny, brief contact awakening an aching sensation deep inside her.

No! Desperately she tried to impose some order on whirling thoughts. She had to think of something, *anything*, to distract herself from the dangerous path her mind was taking. Something very ordinary. Perhaps she should try counting backwards from a hundred; that had never failed to send her to sleep in the past. Ninety-nine, ninety-eight . . .

But, although she tried every trick in the book, nothing worked and she stirred again restlessly, turning towards the middle of the bed.

'What's wrong?'

Ginny was concentrating so hard that the quiet question startled her, her eyes flying open to look straight into Ross's blue ones, unnervingly only inches away from her. He was half lying, half sitting up, his head propped up on one hand, his elbow on the pillow, and for all that he had declared that he needed to sleep he still looked very wide awake.

'Can't you sleep?'

The shadows in the room hid the expression in his eyes, but Ginny was stunned to hear a note of what sounded like genuine concern in his voice.

'I—can't get comfortable.'

That was only too true. Lying here beside him like this, feeling the way she did, had to be one of the most uncomfortable experiences she had ever had in her whole life.

'You must ache after that fall. I should have—'

'No,' Ginny cut in hastily. If she felt like this just lying next to him, how would she feel if he was to touch her? 'I'll be fine,' she managed through a dry throat that made the words come out in a hoarse croak.

Ross's eyes were just deep, dark pools in the dim light, and Ginny found she couldn't drag her own gaze away, couldn't move even when he reached out a hand and gently touched her hair.

'Poor Ginny.' His voice was soft, almost a caress in itself. 'Where does it hurt?' His hand moved to her shoulder, the strong fingers kneading the bruised muscle with a light pressure that was soothing and rhythmically hypnotic. 'Here?'

The only sound Ginny could manage was a wordless murmur that might have been agreement as she found herself leaning back against his hand, enjoying the ease it brought to her aching neck and shoulders.

'That's better, is it?'

She heard his words as if through a thick fog, her mind refusing to concentrate on anything beyond the relief and pleasure his hands were bringing her, and a sigh escaped her as the caressing fingers moved slowly down her back.

'Things aren't as bad as they seem,' Ross murmured. 'At least, they don't have to be—'

His hands stilled suddenly as he looked deep into her eyes.

'You're a very lovely lady,' he whispered, his face so close to hers that she felt the warmth of his breath on her cheek. 'You make me want to—'

Ginny knew what was coming, but those dark eyes still held her mesmerised as Ross lowered his head and his lips brushed hers very lightly. Immediately it was as if someone had flicked a switch that sent a current of electricity running through her body, making every nerve-end quiver and obliterating all sense of reality, so that it was Ginny herself who lifted her arms and linked them round his neck, drawing his head down even closer.

She heard a soft murmur of delight and didn't know if it had come from Ross or herself as the pressure of his lips on hers increased, becoming warmly sensual, drawing from her a response that was purely instinctive, no thought beyond physical enjoyment touching her mind. Her whole body seemed to have melted in the warmth of his embrace, and she wriggled closer, flickers

of fire running through her veins as she felt the strength
of his body against her own softness.

Ross's hands were moving again, tracing small, erotic
patterns on her back, the warmth of his touch reaching
her through the thin material of the pyjama jacket,
sending waves of delight washing over her so that even
her toes curled in response. The world, the events of the
day, even the room in which they lay seemed to have
faded to nothingness; there was only herself and this man
and the pleasure they were creating between them.

She felt those strong hands move round to the front
of her body, pausing teasingly just below the curves of
her breasts, then slide down to where the short jacket
ended, exposing the soft skin of her thighs. The light,
warm caress of his fingertips made her breath escape in
a gasp of excitement, and she writhed sensuously, adrift
on a sea of sensation.

'Hell and damnation!'

Ross's explosive curse slashed through the heady haze
in her mind. She felt him tense against her and then,
with a fierce movement, he wrenched himself away from
her, twisting round to lie on his back, staring straight
up at the ceiling.

The cold, lost feeling that pervaded her body brought
Ginny perilously close to tears. Tentatively she reached
out a hand towards Ross, then immediately snatched it
back, trembling all over. What on earth had possessed
her? Only a short time before she had warned this man
to keep away from her, had told him she would rather
die than be touched by him, and yet she had gone into
his arms so willingly, without a thought for her own
safety or the possible consequences. She had to be out
of her mind!

'Poor Ginny.' An echo of Ross's words, his softly husky voice, sounded in her head and she felt sick, a sour, bitter taste in her mouth as she realised what he had done. He had played on her feelings, manipulating her every bit as easily as he had Jamie when he had assured the little boy that there was nothing to worry about.

'That wasn't supposed to happen.' Ross's voice was harsh, rough-edged, and it acted like a dash of icy water in her face, bringing her back to sanity with a shock.

'It certainly wasn't!' High and tight with reaction, the voice she heard sounded quite unlike her own. She couldn't believe that she could sound so hard and brittle. 'I believe that I told you to keep your distance—and I meant what I said. Just keep your wandering hands to yourself in future!'

That brought him upright sharply, the blue eyes dark with some emotion that the shadows in the room made it impossible to read.

'Don't try that one, my beauty! Mine weren't the only hands wandering around here. Only a block of wood could have resisted the invitation in your—'

'*Invitation?*' Ginny spluttered. 'I don't know what——'

'Oh, yes, you do. It was written all over your face. You were begging to be kissed—touched—and I'm not made of wood, I'm very human.'

'*Human?*'

Ginny's temper boiled over. Shock and disbelief at her own reactions combined with a queasy, disturbed sensation in the pit of her stomach to light a volcano of fury in her mind. What made matters so much worse was the fact that she couldn't honestly deny his accusation of inviting his kisses. After the trials and stresses of the day, she had *needed* to hear that note of concern

in someone's voice, needed to be held. In that moment
of weakness, had her vulnerability shown on her face?
And, being the man he was, Ross had interpreted it in
his own selfish way, using it to his advantage.

'You're not human—you're a lousy, filthy sewer rat—
and as for inviting you to touch me—I—I can't think
of anything I wanted less! You disgust me!'

'Sure.' The single, sardonic syllable broke in on her
tirade. 'I noticed you pulling back—fighting me.' The
dark irony of his tone stung like the flick of a whip.
'You were making the pace, lady.'

He glared down into her wide, shocked brown eyes,
and instinctively Ginny shrank back on the pillow, terrified by the barely controlled fury she could see behind
his bitter humour. With a shocking suddenness Ross's
expression changed abruptly. The dark anger faded from
his face and he pushed back the lock of black hair that
had fallen over his forehead with a disturbed gesture.

'Oh, what the hell—?' he muttered, half to himself.
'Look, it's best we forget the whole damn thing. Put it
down to tiredness.'

'Tiredness?' Ginny exclaimed satirically, unable to
control the stabbing sensation of disappointment that
caught her unawares. To have thought that he had found
her attractive, that, being in bed with her like this, he
had been unable to resist trying it on, that she could
have coped with; but to say that he hadn't been thinking
clearly because he was *tired*——

She would have gone on, wanting to tear him to pieces,
verbally at least, but something in his face stopped her
in her tracks. He *did* look tired suddenly; there were
lines of strain around his nose and mouth, and it wasn't
just the dim lighting in the room that had put those
shadows under his eyes.

'Forget it, Ginny.' Weariness threaded Ross's tone, making it dull and flat. 'Just go to sleep.'

If there had been little chance of that before, there was even less now, Ginny thought, but nevertheless, and partly to avoid seeing that disturbing expression on his face, she turned on her side and tried to compose herself if not to sleep then at least to lie still. Her brain was a blur of conflicting emotions, anger, fear and despair combining with her own disgust and disbelief at the way she had responded to Ross, her own tiredness from her mind. What was it about this man that made her behave in a way that was so totally alien to the person she believed herself to be? Never before had she lost control so completely. He *was* an attractive man, it was true, but then so was Mike, the man she had been seeing lately.

Mike! Ginny stiffened in shock at the realisation that in the turmoil of the day she had forgotten all about Mike. She was supposed to be seeing him tonight—last night, she amended ruefully, recalling that it was now well into Thursday morning. Mike Arnold was a photographer for the local newspaper. They had first met when Ginny had opened her agency and Mike had been sent to cover the event. From that initial meeting a friendship had grown, and lately they had been seeing a lot of each other.

With an effort Ginny stilled an urge to move restlessly, supremely conscious of Ross's still form beside her. Was he asleep? She didn't know and she didn't intend taking the risk of finding out. She had had just as much as she could take of Ross Hamilton tonight. Determinedly she turned her thoughts back to Mike. He would think she had stood him up when she hadn't appeared at the restaurant as they had arranged. Her fingers clenched into tight fists, her nails digging into her palms, at the thought of how Ross Hamilton had messed up one more part of her life.

She tried to picture Mike's face, but instead of his burly, blond-haired figure, the only image that floated before her eyes was that of a dark man with a fine, determined mouth and blue eyes that seemed to burn into her.

Damn him to hell! she thought furiously, but deep inside she knew that most of her anger was directed at herself. In all the time she'd known Mike, never once had she been tempted to behave with the abandonment that had gripped her tonight. She enjoyed his company, liked to be kissed and held by him, but it was a comfortable, safe feeling, nothing like the whirlwind of sensation that had assailed her when Ross had touched her.

If only she had managed to escape from the window, as she had planned! She could have been miles away by now, perhaps reporting her story to the police. They could have been back here before Ross had even noticed she had gone. The children would have been restored to their father and she would never, ever have to set eyes on Ross Hamilton again.

And how would she feel about that? an unwelcome, insidious little voice whispered inside her head. Ginny found that the answer didn't come easily, and that frightened her. It should have sprung into her mind at once. She should have felt relieved, overjoyed at the thought of being well away from him, free from him forever, but instead something that felt disturbingly like a pang of regret twisted deep inside her at the prospect of a future without Ross in it.

In spite of the warmth of the bed and Ross's body so close to hers, Ginny suddenly felt terrifyingly, shiveringly cold. She had suspected that Jamie was developing a dose of hero-worship towards Ross, but she had never paused to consider that she might be attracted to him herself. It was foolish, irrational, it went against all laws of logic, and her common sense cried out in outrage against it, but in her heart she knew that she had to face the truth. She had to get away from here as quickly as possible—and not just for Jamie and Lisa's sake. The possible repercussions in her own life if she remained trapped in this house with Ross were far too devastating to contemplate.

Was Ross asleep? Emerging from her disturbed thoughts, Ginny was suddenly very conscious of the silence around her. Ross lay completely still at her side and, listening hard, all she could hear was his relaxed, regular breathing. Her heart lurched in excitement. He *was* asleep—and on the chair at the end of the bed lay the jeans he had discarded—with the keys to the house in their pocket!

Moving with infinite care, she inched towards the edge of the bed. Please God, please let him not wake, she prayed silently, every muscle taut, every nerve alive to the slightest sound or movement as she eased back the blankets. Ross did not move as she swung her feet to the ground. The chair was only a few feet away. Surely she could——

'Don't try it.'

With a choking cry of alarm Ginny spun round. Ross's dark head rested on the pillow, but his eyes were wide open, watchful and alert to her every move. For a second she hesitated, wondering if, even now, she could dash to the chair and retrieve the keys before he could reach her.

'You can forget that idea,' Ross said calmly, interpreting her thoughts with uncanny accuracy. 'I took the precaution of removing the keys before I got into bed.'

He slid his hand under the pillow and Ginny caught the faint clink of metal against metal as he gathered the keys up into his hand. A cry of despair welled up inside her, and she had to bite down hard on her lower lip to prevent it from escaping.

'I did warn you I was a very light sleeper.' Ross's tone was one of exaggerated patience that set Ginny's nerves on edge, making her grit her teeth. 'So why don't you see sense and come back to bed like a good girl?'

'Damn you! Don't patronise me!'

'I'm not patronising, merely practical,' Ross remarked mildly. 'It's some godforsaken hour of the night, and we're both tired. Now, get back in this bed before I come over there and carry you here myself!'

The sudden sharpening of his tone left Ginny in no doubt that he meant what he said, and as she had no desire to repeat the experience of earlier that night she acknowledged bitterly that she had no alternative but to obey him. It was a struggle to force herself to slide into the bed beside him, holding her body stiffly away from any contact with his.

'You really should try to sleep,' Ross told her, once more using that infuriatingly reasonable tone. 'And you know what they say—things always look a lot better in the morning.'

He was wrong about that, Ginny thought miserably, quite wrong. There was no way the coming of morning was going to change anything. She would still be here—and so would Ross. She had never felt so alone or so afraid in her whole life, and the cold light of day would only bring home to her just how bad things were.

CHAPTER SIX

'How much longer are we staying here?'

It was the question Ginny had been dreading, and she was frankly surprised that it had taken Jamie so long to get round to asking it. It was the fourth day of their captivity, and she was in the children's room helping Lisa to dress when Jamie turned to her with the query that left her completely speechless.

How did she answer that? She had asked herself exactly the same question a hundred times. *Why* hadn't Gavin or the police tracked them down by now? She had been so sure that Marshall would immediately suspect his brother-in-law's involvement in the children's disappearance and that that fact would lead to their being found quickly—but of course Gavin had said he had no idea where Ross was living.

'I—I'm not sure. A few days, perhaps. It depends on Ross.'

'*Uncle* Ross,' Lisa corrected automatically, and Ginny had to bite her lip against the rejection of the name that almost escaped her.

She had become increasingly worried by the way the children had taken to Ross, taking his affectionate uncle act at face value. Probably they saw him as a link with their dead mother, and in their innocence were completely unaware of his ulterior motives for bringing them here. What sort of an uncle had he been when his sister was alive? Ginny's thoughts went back to the time, a couple of days earlier, when she had snatched a few moments when Ross was out of the room—something that happened very rarely because he had almost always been there, a darkly oppressive, watchful presence that preyed on her nerves—to try a few careful questions.

'Did you see much of your uncle before—' She had caught herself up hastily. 'When you lived in America?'

'He came to visit us,' Jamie had answered.

'And he took us to the beach,' Lisa had put in. 'It was lots of fun.'

'But that was before Mummy——'

Jamie had broken off abruptly and, seeing his white, shaken face, Ginny had abandoned her questions, folding him in her arms and holding him tightly. When Lisa had tugged at her sleeve, she'd included the little girl in the hug, too, and for a long moment there had been silence, while in her mind Ginny had cursed Ross for inflicting this extra stress on children who had already been through so much.

'Uncle Ross asked me questions about you, too,' Jamie had said at last, his voice muffled by her enclosing arms, and instinctively Ginny had stiffened.

'What sort of questions?' It had been an effort to keep her voice calm and even.

'He wanted to know if I liked you, and I said you're our friend—our special friend. You are, aren't you, Ginny?'

Ginny had only been able to nod, too choked to speak. The two children had won her heart from the first moment she had seen them, and the events of the past few days had enhanced that initial feeling.

'And he said, did Daddy like you, too?'

'What—what did you say?' Ginny had asked carefully.

'I said you were Daddy's special friend, too—that's why you looked after us when Daddy went to work.'

Briefly Ginny had closed her eyes, afraid that what she was feeling might show in them. She could hear Ross's voice saying, 'My dear brother-in-law happens to be the man I most detest in the whole world,' as clearly as if he was standing beside her, and could well imagine that he wouldn't feel too kindly disposed towards anyone who was Gavin's 'special friend'.

'I'm not exactly your father's friend——'

'But he likes you a lot!' Jamie had insisted. 'I know he does. He told Mrs Hayes he didn't know what he'd have done without you. He said you were an angel——'

It was at that point that the faint sound of movement had alerted Ginny, and she had looked up to see Ross standing in the doorway, an unreadable expression on his face. As soon as he realised she was watching him his face had changed, becoming the cold, hard mask she had come to dread.

'So we won't be going back to Daddy's?' Jamie's voice dragged her back to the present.

'Not yet.'

She tried hard to iron the concern from her voice. Jamie and Lisa had been amazingly well-behaved so far, but she hated to think what might happen when the novelty of the 'surprise holiday' wore off and they began to feel homesick and want their father.

'I'm *glad*!' Lisa declared, startling Ginny, who had expected a completely different response.

'Me, too,' Jamie put in. 'I don't want to go back there. I don't like it—and I don't like our new Mummy.'

Ginny's eyes went to the little boy's face, seeing an unexpected and unchildlike determination stamped on it. She had only met Gavin Marshall's fiancée once, and had to admit that she hadn't taken to the woman. Miss

Blythe was an elegant, sophisticated socialite, pretty enough—in fact some people might have described her as beautiful with her sleek cap of coppery hair and bright green eyes, but there had been a hard, brittle quality about her that had alienated Ginny from the start. She couldn't see the other woman taking too happily to being stepmother to two young children; in fact, Miss Blythe looked anything but the motherly type that Jamie and Lisa clearly needed.

Ginny's thoughts went back to the occasion when she had brought the children back to the house to find Gavin Marshall's fiancée waiting for them. She had barely spared a glance for the painting Lisa had brought home from school, and had sent the children straight up to the nursery, declaring that she didn't want them messing up the house before their father came home. When the little girl had tried to tell her something about her day, she had snapped sharply that she didn't have time for this right now, though to Ginny's eyes it was obvious that she had nothing more important to do than to finish the glossy fashion magazine she had been reading when they had arrived.

'She's horrid,' Lisa added bluntly. 'She never plays with us like you and Uncle Ross do, Ginny, and she doesn't like us being there when she's with Daddy.'

'And she's *not* our Mummy.'

Jamie's bottom lip showed a worrying tendency to quiver betrayingly, and Ginny's heart went out to the two small children who found it so hard to adjust to all the changes in their lives—not the least of which was the imposition of a stepmother that clearly neither of them found in the least sympathetic.

Perhaps this was why, starved of affection, they had been so quick to accept Ross, because, whatever else she might think of him, Ginny had to admit that where the children were concerned she could find no fault with Ross's behaviour. He had showed surprising patience and a totally unexpected ability to create games to keep Jamie and Lisa occupied—no small problem when they had been confined in this house for so long without once setting foot outside. The first two days had been relatively easy, the weather having changed from the mellow sunshine of the Wednesday to a heavy downpour that would have kept them inside anyway, but yesterday had been fine and dry again.

Ginny remembered the moment on the previous morning when Jamie, bored with the toys, had turned to Ross.

'Can we go out to play? I want to play football.'

Ginny's eyes flew to Ross's face. She was curious to know just how he'd get out of this. Her glance was met by a distinctly sardonic look, one dark eyebrow lifting challengingly.

'I'm afraid the grass is too wet and muddy for you to play on it,' he said smoothly. 'But the hall's pretty big,' he added, seeing the first signs of mutiny in Jamie's pouting bottom lip. 'And it's not been decorated or anything yet. Why don't you play in there? It's big enough to kick a ball about in.'

The compromise had proved acceptable, and later Ross himself had joined in the game, acting as goalkeeper at the foot of the stairs. Hearing the laughter that echoed round the house, seeing Jamie's bright eyes, Ginny had felt a queasy sensation in her stomach at the thought of the growing friendship between the boy and the man who gave every impression of being the affectionate uncle he claimed to be, but whose façade of warmth hid a calculating and unforgiving mind.

The sick feeling grew as she pictured the two of them as she had seen them the night before, when Jamie had refused to let her put him to bed, insisting on having Ross read him his bedtime story. Ross had lounged on the bed at Jamie's side, his long legs stretched out on the red and white bedspread, his arm around the little boy's shoulders while Jamie leaned confidently against the man's strong chest. She would have given anything to be able to march into the room, snatch the book from Ross's hands, and shout at him to get out—to leave the children alone. But one look at Jamie's contented face had forced her into frustrated silence, though she quailed inside at the thought of the time when all this pretence would come to an end, when Jamie must inevitably face the disillusionment of discovering the truth about his new-found hero.

'I like this dress. Don't you think I look pretty?' Lisa's voice intruded into Ginny's thoughts as the little girl twirled round in front of the mirror, eyeing her reflection with precocious satisfaction as she held out the soft pink material of her flared skirt.

'You look like a princess.'

The answer came from the doorway, bringing Ginny's head swinging round to where Ross lounged indolently against the wall. Meeting the silent challenge of her gaze, he smiled easily, that mocking gleam lighting the darkness of his eyes.

'I came to see if you were ready for breakfast.'

And to check that we weren't trying to climb out of any windows, Ginny was tempted to snap back, but, mindful of two small people with very big ears, she swallowed down the retort, silently suffering the sense of prickling unease that always plagued her in Ross's presence. He had been like a constant shadow over the past days, those clear blue eyes watching every move she made until she was ready to scream with tension, hating the feeling that her life was no longer her own, that she hardly dared breathe without checking first to see if Ross's face wore the ominous frown that warned of his disapproval.

'Do you really think I look like a princess, Uncle Ross?' Lisa's innocent chatter broke the silence that seemed to crackle with electricity as she ran towards the doorway.

Ross caught her up and swung her high above his head.

'You're the most beautiful princess I've ever seen,' he assured her with a smile that, even to Ginny's prejudiced eyes, looked totally convincing, making her think of Lisa's story of the trip to a beach in America.

That was the sort of thing you would expect from a caring uncle, but anyone who loved the children would put their interests first, and everything Ross had said showed that the one thing that was foremost in his mind was his hatred of Gavin Marshall and his determination to hurt the other man, without a care for what Jamie and Lisa felt.

'Thank you for choosing this dress—I love it! And I love you too, Uncle Ross.'

Ginny had to look away, her teeth digging into her lower lip as, back on the ground again, Lisa flung her arms around Ross's leg, which was as high as she could reach, and gave him an enthusiastic hug. She could not stand much more of this.

'Breakfast-time, I think,' she said briskly, moving forward to unfasten Lisa's clinging hands, keeping her eyes on the little girl and refusing to look into Ross's face, knowing only too well the mocking triumph she would see there. It had been there on the first morning when, to her complete consternation, he had produced several sets of clothes for the children, all brand new, and of such a perfect fit that they had to be more than just a lucky guess.

How had he known what sizes to buy? She doubted if Sam, devoted father though he was, would have been capable of buying his sons' clothes without some firm advice from her sister. Ross's actions revealed more than careful planning; they were those of a man who, for whatever reason, had taken a very close interest in his nephew and niece.

'It's a pity you didn't have any clothes for Auntie Ginny, too.'

Ginny grimaced wryly, not liking that 'Auntie Ginny' at all. It linked her too closely with Ross, something that made her feel physically ill just to think of it. She wouldn't have been human if her distaste hadn't also been mixed with a strong dose of chagrin at the way Lisa's words caused Ross's eyes to skim over her assessingly, bringing home to her the fact that she was looking very far from her best.

After her escape attempt, her clothes had been completely unwearable and she had been forced to make do with a pair of Ross's jeans and one of his shirts. The shirt swamped her and the jeans had had to be rolled up at the ankles and belted tightly around her slim waist until she felt that the whole effect was unflatteringly similar to the costume of a circus clown.

But what did her appearance matter? At least she was adequately covered, which would be vital if she ever got another chance to escape, a consideration which had helped her to overcome the repugnance she felt at the thought of wearing anything that belonged to Ross. There had been another consideration, too, one that came strongly to mind now as, seeing Ross's eyes rove over her in insolent appraisal, she recalled the events of that first night. Remembering his huskily sensual voice murmuring, 'You're a very lovely lady,' and with Gavin Marshall's condemnation of his brother-in-law echoing in her thoughts, she had resolved that from now on it was imperative to look as drab and unattractive as possible so as to avoid a repetition of the unwanted caresses she had been subjected to.

An unwelcome little voice inside her head reminded her that those caresses hadn't been quite as unwanted as she might like to believe, destroying her mental equilibrium. Her confusion increased as Ross spoke.

'Ah, but Auntie Ginny doesn't need special clothes to make her look beautiful.' The laughter in his voice and the subtle emphasis on that 'Auntie' grated on Ginny's already raw nerves. 'She'd look stunning in an old sack.'

Blue eyes glinting with unconcealed mockery slid to her face.

'Or in——'

None too sure exactly how far he would take this line, Ginny broke in on him swiftly.

'Flattery will get you nowhere, Mr Hamilton!'

'Not *flattery*,' Ross parried promptly, with an expression of hurt innocence that had her clasping her hands together tightly as she fought off the urge to wipe it from his face. 'Flattery is exaggeration, and I was telling the simple truth—and it's Ross, remember.'

Unable to think of a suitably crushing reply that wouldn't shock their two small companions, Ginny took refuge in practicalities instead, busying herself with getting the children downstairs and then filling two bowls with cereal for Jamie and Lisa with a fair assumption of calm, though she prayed that Ross couldn't see the way her hand shook as she poured the milk.

It was impossible to decide which she hated most—the cold, hard man who had confronted her on that first day, or the tormenting, mocking creature he had since become. She detested both of them, but that first man had been easier to handle than this new Ross, because now she had no idea which way he was going to jump, and he constantly pulled the rug out from under her feet with the sort of remark that in anyone else she would have considered flirtatious, but which, coming from Ross, was just plain infuriating.

Ross's words reminded her of things she would far rather forget, like the nights she had spent in his bed, wearing only that embarrassingly revealing pyjama jacket. For the past two nights she had stayed up as late as she possibly could, deciding that the hours spent downstairs in Ross's uncomfortable company were at least preferable to the time when she had to share his bed. As a result she had crawled upstairs totally exhausted and had been profoundly grateful for the sleep that had claimed her almost immediately, so that she had lain like the dead, oblivious to Ross's presence, only surfacing when he got up—which was always bright and early, well before the children woke. She had been terrified of a repetition of her reaction of that first night, panic-stricken at the thought of what might happen if Ross was to touch her again, and was deeply relieved at the way he seemed to be following her lead in pretending that that night had never happened—except for those infuriatingly frequent flirtatious remarks that she knew were only meant to goad her into losing her temper.

'Uncle Ross, can we play outside today?' Jamie had gulped down his breakfast and was eager to get away from the table.

'I'm afraid not.'

This time, Ross's refusal was no subterfuge in order to make sure the children weren't seen; the rain lashing the windows made it only too clear that it was not a day for anyone to be outside.

'But you can use the hall again, if you like—but only the hall.'

'And will you play goalie again?'

Ross's smile threatened to turn Ginny's sense of reality upside-down and inside-out. She knew how much Gavin Marshall feared this man's influence on his children, but over the past few days she had found it impossible to equate the man her employer had described with the tolerant warmth Ross had displayed towards the children. Sometimes it seemed as if he was two totally different men. But one of those men was the one who had so heartlessly taken the children away from their father, and that fact, and his own declaration that Gavin was the man he most detested in the world, must always sway her to Gavin's side.

'OK, I'll be there in a minute—but first I want to have a word with Ginny.'

That remark had Ginny stiffening in apprehension. Since the first night she had tried her hardest to avoid any direct conversation with Ross, concentrating on the children when they were awake and determinedly switching on the television in the evenings, assuming an interest in programmes she neither saw nor heard, thankful that Ross, too, addressed only the most necessary remarks to her, keeping those to the strictest minimum, although always taking great care to remember that they had to convince Jamie and Lisa that nothing was wrong. Perhaps he had swallowed her story of an imaginary fiancé, after all.

But what did he want to talk to her about now? She was damned sure she didn't want to hear a word he said, and there wasn't a single thing she wanted to say to him— nothing that was in the least bit ladylike, anyway. With an abrupt movement she pushed back her chair and, her movements awkward and jerky because every nerve was stretched as tight as a bow-string, began flinging the breakfast dishes into the sink with deliberate disregard for whether she cracked them or not.

'Ginny, I think it's time we had a talk—Ginny!' Ross raised his voice against the clatter she was making.

'I heard you!' Ginny turned on the tap with unnecessary force so that the water poured into the sink in a torrent, creating a spectacular display of bubbles. 'But I don't think we've got anything to talk about—unless you're going to tell me you've decided to let us go.'

She turned to him, unable to hide the foolish hope in her eyes, but wasn't really surprised when he shook his head firmly.

'That isn't possible, I'm afraid.'

His smile was wry and, despite herself, Ginny felt a tug of attraction as she acknowledged how much she had missed that smile. He had been so quiet and withdrawn over the past few days that she had forgotten how devastatingly charming he could be when he wanted.

Furious with herself at the way she had let her guard slip, revealing, even if it was only to herself, a chink in the armour she had tried to build up around herself, she turned back to the washing-up bowl and began to scrub egg from a plate with such force that it threatened to remove the pattern as well.

'Look, why don't you leave that? Sit down and have another cup of coffee——'

'I don't want another coffee.' With a struggle, Ginny put her mental armour back in place. 'And I don't want to sit down. I hate lingering round a table littered with dirty plates and cups, and if I sit around in this house much longer I shall go stark raving mad!'

'It's funny,' Ross put in. 'I wouldn't have put you down as the domesticated type.'

'And what would you know about it?' Ginny flashed back. 'Oh—I forgot—you've been spying on me.'

The thought turned her stomach. How long had she been going about her life, unaware of the fact that his coldly prying eyes were on her?

'Not spying on you, Ginny.' Ross's voice was unexpectedly quiet. 'I knew about you, of course, but it was the children I wanted. Your involvement in all this was just a mistake.'

'Oh!'

Ginny was unable to bite back the instinctive exclamation that rose to her lips as a sudden, sharp pain lanced through her. A *mistake*, that was all she was—a foolish error, an unwanted problem, the one flaw in his carefully thought-out plan. Her precarious grip on her composure slipped as she realised how much his slighting comment hurt.

'This water's too hot,' she added hastily in a desperate attempt to cover up the revealing exclamation, give another reason for it.

'Then leave the bloody washing-up! I'm more than capable of managing it.'

That had been another surprise, Ginny reflected. She had assumed that, having lumbered himself with her, Ross would have been swift to take advantage of the

situation and would have expected her to perform the
traditional female role of cook and general domestic help,
but he had very soon disillusioned her on that score. He
had taken responsibility for everything, including the
meals they ate, and had proved himself more than competent, so much so that she had had to acknowledge
that, even if she hadn't been there, the children would
have been well-fed and kept warm and comfortable.

'I've started, so I'll finish,' she quipped, using flip-
pancy to hide the way she was really feeling, the unexpected pain at hearing herself described as a mistake
having left a dull, bruised feeling deep inside her. 'And,
contrary to your opinion, I quite enjoy being domesticated. Why, at home—'

She broke off abruptly, unable to cope with the wave
of desolation that broke over her at the thought of her
small house, empty for the past four days. The secure
haven it offered now seemed a million miles away.

'At home?' Ross prompted quietly. 'What would you
be doing now?'

What *would* she be doing? Her home and the activi-
ties she pursued there could have belonged to another
world, so that she found it hard even to picture them.
With a sense of shock she realised that it was the
weekend, and remembered what she had had planned.

'Dad gave me a lorry-load of plums from the trees in
his garden. I was going to make them into jam—and
perhaps some chutney.'

'Jam?' Frank disbelief rang in Ross's voice.

'That's right.' The words came out unevenly as Ginny
faced the contrast between the quiet domesticity of the
way she had anticipated spending this weekend with the
nightmarish situation in which she now found herself.
'I know it might seem a false economy, all that work

just for one person, but Dad had such a bumper crop this year and Mum couldn't use them all—and, besides, I enjoy doing it. It's very therapeutic, all that chopping, and I find it so satisfying to see all the jars...'

Her voice faded as she turned and saw the way he was looking at her, those amazing blue eys touched with astonishment and something strangely close to confusion.

'I wonder if you'll ever cease to surprise me,' Ross said slowly. 'I find it very hard to imagine you, of all people, indulging in such an old-fashioned pursuit as jam-making. It's the last thing I would have expected from the elegant——'

'You're making one hell of a lot of assumptions about me!' Ginny snapped, infuriated by the satirical inflection on that 'of all people' which reminded her sharply of the scathing comment he had made about her 'high society life'. He really had an outsize chip on his shoulder about that.

'If they're the wrong assumptions, then put me right.'

The quiet response was the last thing she had expected, and for a moment she could only stare into those clear blue eyes, feeling suddenly as if she could lose herself in their depths. What had happened to the hard, aggressive man she believed—knew him to be? She didn't know; the only thing she did know was that she wanted to keep this Ross with her, wanted to know more about him.

'What—what have you got against Gavin Marshall?' The question came slowly, hesitantly. She was afraid of sparking off an outburst of that dark anger, but she *had* to know. If there was any possible explanation for his actions, she needed to know it, needed it with a desperation that frightened her. Surprisingly, the explosion didn't come.

'The way he treated my sister.' Ross's tone was deep and sombre. 'He really messed up her life.'

With some help from you, a stern sense of reality forced Ginny to add in the privacy of her own thoughts. That incomprehensible rush of longing to know more about him had overwhelmed her, leaving her feeling weak and vulnerable, but she had to keep a cool head, weigh what he said against what Gavin had told her.

'Gavin's no angel when it comes to women.' There was a new and disturbing intensity about the way Ross spoke, and his darkened eyes were fixed on her face. 'In fact, he's a complete bastard——'

'Isn't that rather a case of the pot calling the kettle black?' Rosy colour rushed to Ginny's cheeks as she realised that she'd spoken her thoughts out loud.

To her amazement Ross laughed, the sound warm and mellow, without the harsh cynicism she expected to hear.

'So that's what he told you. Typical Gavin—there never was any love lost between us.'

That had to be the understatement of the year, Ginny thought.

'But why can't you end this stupid feud now—for Jamie and Lisa's sake at least, if not—'

'It's for Jamie and Lisa's sake that I'm doing this,' Ross cut in sharply.

'You could have fooled me! What possible good will it do them to be taken away from their father like this?'

'Listen, lady, let me tell you about Gavin—'

'I don't want to know what Gavin did to *you*! What concerns me is that he can give the children a good home. They have everything they need at the Meridew house——' She broke off abruptly as Ross's violent curse splintered the air.

'Everything they need?' Black cynicism thickened Ross's voice. 'Damn it, Ginny, how can I get rid of those rose-coloured spectacles you're wearing——'

His words were drowned as the children's laughter, which had been a background accompaniment to their conversation suddenly swelled to a new, louder pitch, which was followed by an ominous-sounding crash.

'What have those two terrors done now?'

In the abrupt, stunned silence from the hall, Ross's eyes met Ginny's in a look that expressed all the re-signed exasperation ever felt by an adult when con-fronted by the mischievousness of two boisterous children, all anger wiped from his face, the corners of his mouth twitching into a grin that had her smiling un-thinkingly in response, her own lips curving softly, until the intimacy of the moment dawned on her, sobering her expression instantly.

What had he been going to say before he had been interrupted? It wasn't the mention of Gavin that had put the bite of anger in his voice, he'd answered her earlier question reasonably enough. So had it been the thought of Gavin's money that had once again sparked off that savage temper?

The kitchen door was pushed open hesitantly, and a clearly apprehensive Jamie put his head round it.

'I'm afraid we've had a bit of an accident, Uncle Ross.'

His remark was so obviously an understatement that Ginny had to struggle with the bubble of laughter that rose up inside her and, glancing swiftly at Ross, she saw that he too was clearly having trouble controlling the grin that had threatened to reappear, in spite of his ef-forts to look serious.

'What sort of an accident, Jamie?' he asked, his low voice very faintly unsteady.

'We didn't mean to break it——' Jamie broke off as his sister pushed past him.

'It just happened, Uncle Ross. The ball sort of bounced and it was in the way.'

'What was in the way? No, on second thoughts, I think you'd better show me.'

'I don't understand,' Ginny put in. 'There's nothing in the hall you could break.'

Except perhaps a window, a small, irrespressibly hopeful voice added in the privacy of her thoughts. Would it be too much to hope that it might be a window large enough for her to squeeze through?

'Well, it wasn't 'sactly in the hall,' Lisa admitted reluctantly.

'But I told you to stay in the hall and not to go anywhere else.'

Ross's words brought Ginny up short, all amusement fading, and automatically she reached out to grasp Jamie and Lisa by the hand. His smile earlier had momentarily lulled her dislike and distrust of him, and that was a foolish mistake. He had been patient, amazingly tolerant up to now, but if the children had somehow overstepped the boundaries he laid down his reaction might be very different.

During the brief journey across the hall she found herself tensing in anticipation of the probable explosion, her anxiety increasing when she saw the open door at the foot of the stairs and the shattered remains of what had once been a table-lamp lying on the carpeted floor beyond it. Immediately her grip tightened instinctively on the children's hands.

Because this door had always been kept shut before, Ginny had assumed that, like the bedrooms upstairs, it too was unfurnished. Now she saw that it was a comfortable, booklined study with a solid wooden desk set against the far window. On its polished wooden surface stood a computer and word processor, both clearly of the latest design, the sight of which forced her into a hasty rethink of the earlier assumptions. Whatever Ross planned, clearly money wasn't his motive for kidnapping the children. She had no time to consider the problem any further, because at that moment Jamie spoke, bringing her back to the situation in hand.

'It—was an accident,' he said shakily. Clearly some of her unease had communicated itself to him.

For a long, taut moment Ross surveyed the shambles in total silence, his bright blue eyes the only thing that moved as they went from the mess of glass and pottery on the floor to the football, which had somehow lodged itself on the seat of a nearby chair. Then he turned so abruptly that Ginny flinched instinctively, her mouth drying at the thought of what might happen if he lost control of the dangerous temper she had sensed in him from the first time they had met.

But Ross amazed her by crouching down until he was on the children's eye-level, taking their free hands in his.

'Did I say you could go into this room?' he asked quietly, but with just a touch of sternness which gave his words an added force. 'Jamie?' he prompted when he received no answer.

'No, Uncle Ross.' It was just a whisper.

'No. I've said you could play in the hall or any other room in the house but not this one, haven't I?'

'Yes, Uncle Ross.' The answer came from both children this time, their young faces sober, showing that his words had struck home.

'This room is different. This is my private place. I keep all my special things in here and I don't want them disturbed or damaged. That's fair, isn't it? You wouldn't like it if I went into your room and messed it up or broke your toys, would you?'

Ginny watched transfixed as two small heads, one dark, one fair, moved to signify agreement. Ross had their complete attention, she realised; their hands still rested in hers but only limply, their solemn-eyed gaze concentrated on the man before them—and she was every bit as mesmerised as they were.

'So now do you see why I said you weren't to come in here?'

'Yes, Uncle Ross.' Jamie's voice quavered slightly, but he met Ross's eyes with confidence. 'It was naughty and I'm sorry we broke the lamp.'

'Sorry,' Lisa added like a small echo.

For a moment longer Ross held their eyes with the quiet firmness he had shown from the beginning, then suddenly and unexpectedly he smiled, and as Ginny saw relief flood into Jamie and Lisa's faces she found that she too was smiling in delighted admiration at the way the situation had been handled. Ross had got his message across brilliantly, letting Jamie and Lisa know they had been in the wrong without frightening or upsetting them, that calm, steady voice far more effective than if he had shouted in fury.

'OK, so from now on you stay out of this room—promise?'

'We promise,' the children declared in chorus, Lisa detaching herself from Ginny's hand to wind her arms around Ross's neck, burying her face in his shoulder, and for once Ginny found that the sight of the little girl's obvious affection for him didn't upset her. At this moment, at least, Ross deserved it.

Ross gave Lisa a swift, firm hug, then slowly straightened up, one hand going to rest lightly on Jamie's shoulder.

'Right then, Jamie, you're a big boy—you can go and fetch the brush and dustpan from the kitchen and we'll clear up this mess.'

His face radiant, the little boy hurried to do his bidding, looking for all the world as if a huge burden had been lifted from his shoulders—which, from his child's point of view, it probably had, Ginny reflected. Putting herself in his shoes, she could well imagine how apprehensive he would have felt, and she herself had been distinctly nervous about the way Ross might react. Instead she couldn't fault him at all, and she openly admitted to genuine admiration for the sensitivity he had shown. Her brother-in-law, with nearly ten years' experience of fatherhood behind him, couldn't have done any better, and acknowledging that fact necessitated a swift readjustment of her opinion of Ross as a cruel, unthinking monster. Once more she was forced to consider the fact that all she knew about this man was what she had been told by Gavin—a man who, by his own admission, hated Ross Hamilton violently.

Disturbed by such thoughts, Ginny moved uneasily, drawing Ross's eyes towards her. For a moment he looked blank, as if he had forgotten who she was, and she experienced a flash of hurt pride at the thought that he could so easily dismiss her from his mind when she was so intensely aware of him at every moment.

'That was very well done,' she said, that touch of pique still lingering in her voice to make it sound stiltedly cold and distant. 'You surprised me—I didn't think you understood children that well.'

The swift compression of that attractive mouth into a thin, hard line warned that her words had been a mistake and, thinking back over what she had said, she was forced to admit that she could have put things rather better. Her comment sounded horribly cold and condescending. But before she could add anything to improve matters, reveal her genuine admiration, Ross had turned to Lisa.

'Jamie's a long time fetching that dustpan,' he said, nothing of the icy fury she had seen in his eyes showing in his easy tone. 'Why don't you go and see if you can help him find it?'

As the little girl disappeared in the direction of the kitchen, he swung round to Ginny, white marks of fury etched around his nose and mouth, his eyes just blue chips of ice in his rigid mask of a face.

'What the hell did you think I was going to do?' he demanded harshly. 'Tear the poor kids from limb to limb for one small misdemeanour?'

'I didn't mean that the way it sounded.'

'Then how the hell *did* you mean it? Damnation, woman, I've seen you when I'm with Jamie and Lisa, seen how you rush to intervene when I'm trying to get to know them. Your face closes up if I so much as speak to them, and you constantly find some excuse to get them away from me. Oh, it's been done so very carefully, *so* reasonably. It's time to wash their hands before lunch, or you've found a picture in a book that Jamie *must* see—but I know what you're up to. What is it, lady? Don't you think I'm fit to be with your precious Gavin's kids?'

'I——'

The contrast between Ross's earlier calm handling of the children and this sudden, savage tirade deprived Ginny of the ability to think or speak clearly.

'Well?' The single syllable was flung at her with the force of a bullet from a gun. 'Why are you so determined to keep me away from them?'

'You *know* why! For pity's sake, they're only children, and you're using them in this appalling feud you're waging with their father.'

'Some father!' Ross's voice was a brutal snarl. 'He——'

'Here's the dustpan, Uncle Ross.'

They had been so intent on each other, blue eyes locking with brown, that they hadn't seen Jamie reappear, followed by Lisa proudly holding the brush aloft, and for a second both of them were silent, confused by the unexpected interruption. Ross was the first to recover, switching on a warm smile with a speed and facility that stunned Ginny as he took the dustpan from the little boy's outstretched hand.

'Great. Now we'll soon have this cleared up.'

Ginny watched dazedly as he bent to the task of sweeping up the fragments of the smashed lamp, her mind bruised by the violent volcanic eruption she had just experienced. She couldn't understand Ross's reaction. He had to know that it was cruel to get too close to the children when, one day, with his aim of hurting Gavin Marshall accomplished, he would simply hand them back to their father and probably never see them again after he had used them in this coldly calculating way.

And yet, only moments before, she had admitted to wholehearted admiration for Ross's sensitivity and understanding. Ginny shook her head in confusion. The two sides to Ross's character didn't add up—and during that last, frightening outburst, mixed in with the blazing anger and savage disgust, she was sure she had seen a flash of some raw, deeply felt emotion in those electric blue eyes. It was almost as if he *cared*; as if he had been genuinely hurt by the way she had tried to keep the children away from him.

'Some father,' he had said, and would have expanded on that damning comment if they hadn't been interrupted. She had been desperately concerned about what Gavin might be feeling—but where was the children's father? He had had days in which to find them. The sudden worrying suspicion crept into her mind that, perhaps, instead of asking Jamie about Ross, she should have tried to find out more about *Gavin*.

Ginny's eyes went to Ross's dark head, still bent over the task of clearing up the mess on the carpet. Only a few days before, she had been convinced that he was the most detestable, cruel man she had ever met, but his behaviour towards Jamie and Lisa had slowly eroded that conviction until she no longer knew what she thought or felt. Would she ever understand this man who held her prisoner in his house?

She was suddenly frozen in shock at the realisation that even to think that way meant that she *wanted* to understand Ross. A sensation like the trail of tiny, icy footprints crept down her spine as she recalled the urgent need to know his motives she had experienced such a short time before, and she shivered uneasily as she admitted to herself that, in spite of everything, against every law of common sense or self-preservation, she was drawn to Ross as a needle was attracted to a magnet, and that if she didn't find a way to escape soon she would be trapped in another, very different way, one from which she might never emerge emotionally unscathed.

CHAPTER SEVEN

'No! I don't want to! I don't *want* to!'

The frightened cry, uttered in a shrill, high-pitched voice, penetrated Ginny's sleep sharply, jolting her awake with a jarring suddenness so that for a moment she lay staring in confusion, not knowing what had disturbed her. Then a movement beside her reminded her of just where she was—and with whom. As Ross flung back the bedclothes and swung his feet to the floor, the terrified cry came again.

'Please—*no—I don't want to!*'

Lisa! Realisation flooded into Ginny's sleep-fogged brain, and a moment later she was out of the bed and hurrying across the landing to the children's room.

Ross was there before her. By the time she came through the door he was already on the bed, gathering the small body up into his arms, his deep voice soft and soothing as he murmured calming words.

'Hush, little one, it's all right. It was just a nasty dream——'

Ginny halted in the doorway, transfixed by the sight before her. One swift glance at the other bed was enough to reassure her that Jamie still slept soundly, in spite of the disturbance, and after that she couldn't drag her eyes away from Ross and Lisa as the little girl's eyes fluttered open and she stared dazedly up into Ross's face.

'Uncle Ross?'

It was just a whisper, in such a shaken, terrified voice that Ginny's heart twisted in compassion.

'I'm here, sweetheart,' Ross assured the child softly. 'You had a bad dream, but it's all over now. You're quite safe.'

'Oh, Uncle Ross!'

Lisa's slight body shook convulsively, and tears slid from her eyes and trickled down her cheek. Ross wiped them away with a gentle hand.

'It's all right, lovey. I'm here with you—and so's Ginny.'

'Ginny?'

As Lisa's dark head turned in her direction, Ginny found herself able to move at last and she stepped forward, taking the child's hand in her own as she perched on the bed on the opposite side to Ross.

'Don't cry, darling.'

She aimed for the quiet, soothing tone Ross had used, but wasn't quite successful. The shock of her sudden awakening still lingered, and matters weren't helped by the swift, searching glance Ross had turned on her, the glint of something dangerous showing in their blue depths as he silently challenged her to interfere now, to say something that would draw Lisa away from him.

But there was no way she could do that, not this time. Lisa was barely awake, her wide blue eyes still misted with tears as she cuddled thankfully up against Ross's broad chest, her other hand clutching his fiercely as if she never wanted to let go. It would be too cruel to try to get her away from Ross at the moment; the little girl needed all the comfort she could get, and from the look of things Ross was well able to provide that comfort, his strong arms holding her tight as he stroked her hair and face with gentle movements, all the while murmuring reassurance in that soft, caressing voice that did strange things to Ginny's heart, making it beat unevenly so that her breathing was jerky and disturbed.

After his furious outburst that morning, Ross had barely spoken a word to her. He had strictly avoided any contact with her other than that which was necessary in the practical concerns of caring for two young children, and Ginny had been profoundly grateful for the way he had kept his distance. She had needed some time to get her thoughts back into focus, to impose some order on her feelings, because the very fact that she *had* feelings other than hate and disgust where Ross was concerned made simply being in the same room with him almost impossible to handle.

'Are you feeling better now?' Ross's quiet voice broke in on her thoughts. 'Do you want to tell me about the dream?'

A small shake of her head was all Lisa could manage, and she buried her face in Ross's shoulder, the instinctive movement making an unexpected and infinitely disturbing flash of feeling lance through Ginny, one she recognised with a jarring sense of unreality as that of jealousy. *She* wanted to do just that, wanted to lay all her worries, doubts and fears on a pair of broad shoulders and feel someone's arms come round her, warm and supportive in the way Ross's arms were as they held the little girl.

Someone's? Anyone's? Her mind threw the question at her, and she felt shiveringly cold and then burning hot as she faced the fact that in a brief moment of fantasy she had allowed herself to imagine not just anyone's arms holding her but a particular pair of brown, muscular arms that were now only inches away from where her hand still gripped Lisa's. That realisation made her nerves twist into a thousand tight, painful knots, but the next minute all such worrying thoughts were driven from her mind as she caught Lisa's next words.

'I want my mummy!' Even muffled by the way Lisa's face was still hidden against Ross's shoulder, the words reached Ginny clearly, making her eyes fly to Ross as she stared at him aghast. 'Uncle Ross, I want my mummy!'

'I know, sweetheart, I know. But don't worry, you'll see her very soon.'

Something exploded in Ginny's mind. She couldn't stomach this!

'How can you say that?' she hissed at Ross, fury flaring in her eyes. To let the little girl believe that she would see her mother was the cruellest thing this man had done—the cruellest thing anyone could ever do. Even the obvious need to comfort her didn't justify such an appalling lie. 'That's a terrible——'

'Leave this to me,' Ross cut in on her, his blue eyes clashing with her brown ones over the top of Lisa's dark head. 'I know what I'm doing.'

'No way! I'll not stand by and let you——'

'*Ginny!*' For the first time, Ross's voice rose above that quiet, gentle tone, the hard-edged sound of her name slashing through her words like a sword. 'I think Lisa would like a drink—some warm milk, perhaps. Why don't you go and get her some?'

'And leave her alone with you, a prey to heaven knows what other lies you'll tell her?' Ginny's voice was thick with loathing and disgust, and she tensed in anticipation of the expected eruption, but surprisingly it didn't come.'Don't interfere in things you don't understand.' Each word seemed formed in ice dropping freezingly on Ginny's raw nerves. 'You don't know one half of what's been going on, so I suggest you keep a grip on that over-active tongue of yours and do as I say.'

That 'over-active tongue' was sorely tempted to tell him to go to hell, but one swift glance at those coldly burning blue eyes, the rigid set of his jaw and the way his skin seemed stretched taut over the harsh cheekbones, forced Ginny to admit to second thoughts. Now wasn't the time to have this out with him; Lisa was far too vulnerable, she couldn't put her through any more. But still she couldn't abandon the little girl to Ross's dubious attentions. Her own jaw set stubbornly and she lifted her chin defiantly.

'Why don't you fetch the milk yourself?'

She was stunned to see the muscles at the corners of his hard mouth twitch as if he was having difficulty suppressing a smile, but there was no corresponding lightening of his eyes; they remained as icy cold as a winter sky.

'I would if I thought Lisa would let me go, but—'

He moved slightly to demonstrate his point, and immediately Lisa made a small, wordless sound of protest and, snatching her hand from Ginny's, fastened both her arms around his narrow waist, holding him still with all her strength.

Point taken? Ross didn't speak the words, but Ginny could read the message all too clearly in his eyes, her opposition crumbling even further when he followed it up by saying, 'This isn't the time or the place to argue this out. The last thing Lisa needs is any further upset, and as you've gone to some pains to make sure of that yourself I'm sure you'll appreciate that point. The most important thing is to get her back to sleep. Then, if you want, you can call me all the abusive names that are so clearly burning a hole in your tongue.'

He waited a nicely calculated moment to give his words time to sink in, then continued in a voice so calmly reasonable that it made Ginny grit her teeth in impotent fury.

'So, now will you go and fetch that milk?'

Ginny knew she was caught in a cleft stick; she had no alternative but to do as he said. How could she do otherwise when Ross had used precisely the same arguments as she had used to herself only moments before? The first consideration *was* that they should get Lisa back to sleep. So she'd fetch that damned milk, but only because *Lisa* needed it. And when the child was asleep, she promised herself—then just you wait, Ross Hamilton!

It took only minutes to warm a pan of milk, but that was long enough for her to consider the possibility of a chance of escape while she was alone downstairs. If she knew Ross, every door and window would be firmly locked, and the keys—she froze suddenly, her hand tightening on the mug—the keys would be under his pillow in the bedroom.

She half turned towards the door, her mind working overtime, considering her chances of getting back upstairs unobserved, but then, reluctantly, turned back, rejecting the idea before it had had time to form fully. She couldn't abandon Lisa now, not while the little girl was still so vulnerable after the horror of the nightmare that had gripped her. She had determined that her presence here would ensure that neither of the children were upset or frightened, and right now that had to be her first priority. With a sigh, she moved to pour the milk into the mug.

Lisa was much calmer by the time Ginny returned to the bedroom to find her sitting quietly in bed, Ross's arm still around her shoulders. Grudgingly Ginny had to admit that whatever Ross had said to the little girl in her absence had certainly worked, though she quailed inside at the thought that he might once more have resorted to the comforting but totally untrue and potentially very damaging promise that she would see her mother again very soon.

Her head held stiffly erect, her features schooled into an expression of composure she was very far from feeling, Ginny handed the mug of milk to Lisa and watched silently as she drank it. She was supremely conscious of Ross's blue eyes watching her with a peculiar intensity, but she stubbornly refused to turn her head in his direction. Her showdown with Ross Hamilton would come later; for now her attention was concentrated on Lisa, and she was glad to see that, having drained the last of the milk, the child settled down in the bed, turning her face into the pillow with every appearance of complete relaxation.

Ross waited a few minutes until Lisa's soft, regular breathing told him she was fast asleep, then, slowly and carefully, he eased himself off the bed and stretched tiredly. The movement drew Ginny's eyes to him at last and she felt a sudden rush of response as she watched his muscles slide under the skin of his broad chest and shoulders. Silently she cursed herself for her involuntary response. She didn't want to find *anything* about this man attractive. She wanted to hate him with all the intensity of which she was capable, because only that way was she safe from the disturbing fascination he seemed to hold for her.

'I want to talk to you,' she said, her inner conflict making the words come out cold and proud.

'I rather thought you would,' was the dry response.

Ross turned to the other bed where, amazingly, Jamie still slept peacefully, oblivious to everything that had been happening around him. With careful hands he drew the blankets up round the boy's still form and tucked them in close to him. The action twisted something deep within Ginny, once more threatening her view of Ross as a cold, uncaring creature, an opinion she desperately wanted to hold on to as if it were a lifeline between herself and her sanity.

'Why don't you go and make some coffee? I'll be down in a minute.'

It was only when she saw Ross turn towards the bedroom that Ginny remembered the keys. Now, too late, she realised that what she should have done was to fetch them anyway and hold them with her, ready for the time when, with Lisa safely asleep, she could have made another escape attempt. But, if she had, would there have been any chance of her using the keys anyway? she asked herself in a mood of bitter realism. Surely the first thing Ross would have done would have been to check that the keys were still where he had left them. Probably that was exactly what he was doing right now. With a despondent sigh she turned and went downstairs.

The kettle had boiled and she was pouring the hot water into mugs by the time Ross joined her in the quiet kitchen. Ginny had spent the few minutes she had been alone rehearsing exactly what she wanted to say to him, going over and over the angry, contemptuous words in her head; but when he finally appeared in the doorway all her carefully thought-out phrases evaporated like mist before the sun, and she could only stand silently, waiting for him to make the first move.

'Here——' Ross held something out to her, and dimly Ginny recognised it as the while towelling robe she had worn on the first night after her abortive escape attempt. 'I thought you might need this. It's pretty cold and——'

His eyes slid down from her face, wandering over her body in a slow, lingering gaze that was almost a caress.

'And you haven't much on.' His voice had a strange, husky note in it, one that he had clearly made an effort to erase when he spoke again, more briskly. 'I've lit the fire in the living-room too; it'll soon warm the place up.'

His last words were just a blur to Ginny because that look had brought home to her the fact that she was wearing only the short blue pyjama jacket, a fact that earlier events had driven completely from her mind. Now she couldn't be more aware of how little protection the skimpy garment afforded her from that blue-eyed gaze that seemed to sear across her exposed flesh, leaving a fiery trail where it had touched.

With an abrupt movement she snatched the robe from Ross's hands and pulled it on, her fingers clumsy and awkward as a result of the wave of hot embarrassment that swept through her. She had worn the pyjama jacket every night since Ross had first given it to her, but she had always put it on in the privacy of the bathroom and then hurried under the protective covering of the bed-clothes before Ross came upstairs. Never before had she been exposed to that keenly assessing gaze in such skimpy attire for such a length of time.

With the robe securely fastened around her waist she felt much more secure, some of her confidence returning to unfreeze her tongue, so that she was able to say, 'Shall we go and sit down, then? I'd like to get this over as soon as possible. I don't know about you, but I would like to get some sleep tonight.'

'So would I,' Ross agreed equably, leading the way into the living-room. 'But I doubt if either of us will get any rest until you've unburdened yourself of all the violent thoughts that are clearly buzzing around inside that pretty head of yours, so why don't you just come straight out with whatever it is you're thinking and then maybe we can sort things out?'

For a moment Ginny simply stared at him, too stunned to form a coherent thought. After the cold anger she had seen burning in his eyes only a short time before, his present easy manner was the last thing she had expected, and the drily humorous tone was in sharp contrast to the violent explosion she had anticipated with a strong degree of apprehension. And that casual compliment had done nothing to ease the nervous racing of her pulse; in fact, it had aggravated the problem, making it suddenly very hard to breathe naturally.

Seeing Ross now as he leaned back in his chair, sipping his coffee appreciatively, his strong body relaxed and his long legs stretched out in front of him, she could hardly believe that he was the same man she had confronted upstairs in the children's bedroom. He had pulled on a pale blue sweatshirt on top of the navy pyjama trousers—a fact for which, initially, she felt grateful because it hid the disturbing effect of that tautly muscled, golden-tanned chest. But, even as she thought that, the more instinctive, less controlled part of her brain was acknowledging the way the blue of the sweatshirt highlighted those vividly coloured eyes, and the way the soft cotton hugged the contours of his powerful torso, emphasising the hardness of the body underneath. Her mouth felt dry and the uneven, jerky thud of her heart made her feel distinctly uncomfortable, even though she tried to put her reaction down to nervousness about the coming confrontation—an argument that, even in her own ears, sounded disturbingly unconvincing.

'Well?' Ross prompted as the silence between them lengthened. 'You had plenty to say upstairs—don't tell me you've changed your mind.'

The thread of satirical amusement that laced his tone set a spark to the fire of anger that other, unwelcome thoughts had banked down to smouldering embers, making it flare up dramatically.

'You know damn well I haven't changed my mind! And I'm damn sure you also know what I want to say. I have every intention of telling you what's on my mind— but I'll do it in my own damn time!'

One dark eyebrow drifted lazily upwards, and a mocking smile curved Ross's lips.

'Three "damns" in as many sentences,' he drawled ironically. 'Obviously bad temper doesn't make for a creative command of the English language.'

For a moment Ginny felt as if someone had punched her hard in the stomach, driving all the breath from her body, but then she caught the taunting gleam in his eyes and anger came to her rescue once more.

'How I say it doesn't matter! I've never seen such a cruel, vicious and thoroughly revolting act as to tell Lisa that she'll see her mother very soon when you know da——'

That glint in his eyes had brightened and she caught herself up hastily.

'When you know only too well that your sister is dead and——'

Her words faltered, died, as she looked into Ross's face. What had she said to put that expression on it? There was no amusement there at all, no light in the blue eyes that were suddenly as dark and unfathomable as

the sea at night. He had lost colour, too: his skin was
pale where it was drawn tight over his cheekbones, and
the hand that gripped his coffee-mug showed white at
the knuckles. So he did have some feelings, after all, and
in mentioning his sister's death she had clearly touched
on a raw spot.

'Who told you that?' Ross demanded so savagely that
Ginny shrank back against the cushions of the settee,
her brown eyes widening in panic. It wasn't anger that
had made his voice so harsh but something else, some
powerful emotion she couldn't even begin to interpret.

'Why, Gavin Marshall, of course.' It was a struggle
to control her voice, and it came and went in the most
disturbing way.

'*Marshall!*' Ross spat the name out, making it a sound
of disgust, his face darkening with anger.

This was the real Ross Hamilton, Ginny thought on
a shiver of fear. She could forget the quietly assured,
relaxed man of moments before, the competent, prac-
tically capable person who had provided those meals and
the clothes for Jamie and Lisa, even the gentle, patient
and understanding man who had handled the children
so well had to be put aside, though she felt as if a knife-
wound of loss had stabbed deep into her heart at the
thought. Ross was at last revealed in his true colours as
a man riddled with bitter hatred—and all that hatred
was directed at the children's father. Dear heaven, what
had Gavin Marshall done to him?

'Yes, Gavin Marshall.'

Ginny lifted her chin defiantly, ruthlessly suppressing
the pangs of regret that tormented her at the thought of
the loss of all those other sides to this man.

'Jamie and Lisa's father. The man you set out to hurt by this whole kidnapping scheme in the first place. I don't know what it is you've got against him——'

'Don't you?' Ross cut in violently. 'Do you really not know what there is between Gavin Marshall and myself? Well, Miss Blythe, I'll tell you, and then maybe——'

He got no further, because Ginny broke in on him sharply. '*What* did you call me?'

Her question created a sudden silence, a silence in which Ginny could feel the effects of her outburst reaching out to enclose them like the ripples created when a stone was thrown into a pond.

'What did you call me?' she repeated more calmly, enunciating each word with careful precision.

'Miss Blythe. That is your name, isn't it? Ginevra Blythe.'

For a moment Ginny didn't recognise the name. Then at the back of her mind she heard Gavin Marshall's voice saying, 'My fiancée, Miss Blythe, will be waiting for the children,' and realisation burst on her so swiftly that she laughed out loud.

'I'm afraid you've got your wires crossed somewhere. I'm not Miss Anything Blythe.'

She had never heard Gavin Marshall's fiancée's first name before, but now that she had she decided that it suited the woman—all show and surface glamour. And Ross's mistake explained so many things—that comment about the ring, his scathing 'your precious Gavin'. But why did Ross think that *she* was Ginevra Blythe?

'But—Jamie said——'

If the effect of her attack about his sister had been dramatic, the result of this declaration was positively devastating. Ross suddenly seemed to have lost all composure. In place of the confident, controlled man she knew, a man totally sure of himself and his actions, she now saw someone thoroughly confused and disconcerted, a man who seemed to have trouble finding the words he needed and whose face was a picture of shock, the blue eyes spectacularly vivid above his pale, drawn cheeks.

Jamie had said she was Gavin's special friend, had reported his father's description of her as an angel, and earlier— Suddenly it was as if she had entered a time-warp and was back on the country road that led to Holme Hall school, with the dark blue Escort blocking the road and Ross standing, tall and darkly threatening beside it.

She could picture Jamie getting out of the car, feel Ross's hard hand encircling her wrist so vividly that unconsciously she rubbed at the place where he had held her as if the bruises still lingered. In her mind she heard Jamie's voice saying, 'Ginny!' and saw once again how Ross's face had changed, becoming coldly distant. Ginny—Ginevra.

'Oh, yes, my name's Ginny, but it's *not* short for Ginevra. It's Virginia, but no one ever calls me that. Virginia Fletcher.'

She could see it all now. Once she knew the facts, it was easy to understand and it explained the mystery over Ross's reasons for taking her with him instead of leaving her behind in the car. Having planned to get at Gavin Marshall by kidnapping his children, he had found that, as he believed, he had also had his enemy's fiancée handed to him on a plate. He must have thought all his birthdays had come at once, imagining the effect the loss of all three of his loved ones would have on his brother-in-law. But he couldn't have spied out the land as well as she had imagined if he hadn't known that Ginevra Blythe was a sleek, petite creature of about thirty, not a tall twenty-four-year-old with a mane of unruly dark auburn curls.

'Do you expect me to believe this?' Ross had regained something of his earlier composure, and his eyes were hard and assessing as they fixed on her face.

'Oh, that's easily proved.'

She glanced around, looking for her handbag, and found it on the floor near her chair. A moment later she had one of the agency's business cards in her hand and held it out to Ross, an irrepressible sense of triumph making her lips curve into a smile as she saw the way his eyes went to the white slip of card and then back to her face, doubt and uncertainty clouding their brightness.

'Domestic Help Agency,' he read aloud, his voice slightly hoarse, his usually confident tones eroded completely. 'Manager——'

'Virginia Fletcher,' Ginny broke in, unable to stop herself.

Then, prompted by a wicked urge to drive the lesson home, she added the address and telephone number that were printed on the card, under her name. The sense of victory was sweet as she saw Ross's lean brown fingers tighten on the white slip, crushing it savagely, and she couldn't resist adding, 'Now do you believe me?'

A slow, silent nod was her only answer, Ross's eyes fixed unseeingly on a point somewhere beyond him, a deep frown creasing his forehead.

That frown punctured Ginny's bubble of triumph, and she had to bite back a small cry of distress as she felt all the delight drain from her like air from a pricked balloon. She had proved she wasn't Ginevra Blythe—but what difference did that make? Ross was still the man who was prepared to use two innocent children in order to hurt their father, and, now that he had discovered she wasn't who he thought she was, was he likely to treat her any more kindly? If he did have a thing about wealth, then her own family's decidedly comfortable situation could well rouse his antipathy every bit as much as Gavin's.

In spite of the heat from the fire, Ginny felt shiveringly cold, as if she was encased in a block of ice as she perched on the edge of her seat, her nerves too tightly stung to enable her to sit more comfortably. When Ross finally turned to her she started nervously, wide, apprehensive brown eyes going to his face in an attempt to read his thoughts in his eyes.

To her consternation, what she saw there wasn't the anger she had feared, nor even contempt. The blue eyes were strangely gentle, and something that looked unbelievably like distress darkened their bright colour. Her confusion deepened further when at last Ross spoke.

'I think I owe you an apology.'

With the image of the anticipated hostile reaction still vivid in her mind, his words were so unexpected that Ginny could only stare in blank amazement.

'I'm desperately sorry that you got mixed up in all this. I'm afraid there's been a case of mistaken identity. I said I'd been planning this for months—but most of that time was spent in tracking Gavin down. I'd only been in Epton for just over twenty-four hours— I hadn't been spying on you as you seemed to think.'

There was a rough-edged urgency in his voice that startled Ginny. It was as if it was vitally important to him that she believed what he said.

'I knew about Marshall's fiancée—that sort of gossip is easy to pick up in a small town. She was a redhead— I was told an arrogant little madam with more money than sense.' His mouth twisted wryly. 'My informant's opinion, not mine. Miss Blythe was none too popular at the local shop. I spent Tuesday afternoon watching the house, and I saw you drive in with Jamie and Lisa—you didn't come out again, though I waited for over an hour.'

Ginny's thoughts went back to Tuesday afternoon, recalling her annoyance when she had returned to the Meridew house to find neither the housekeeper nor Ginevra Blythe at home. Unable to leave the children on their own, she had been forced to phone her office and explain, staying with Jamie and Lisa for almost two hours until Gavin Marshall's fiancée had returned from a shopping trip.

If Ross had stayed perhaps half an hour longer, he would have seen the real Miss Blythe, seen Ginny herself leaving the house to return to the office. And if he had, then perhaps he would have left her behind when he took the children and she would never have been involved in all this. Strangely, that wasn't easy to contemplate. She couldn't imagine never having met Ross Hamilton, never even knowing that he existed. It seemed as if destiny had taken a hand, created the confusion so that they must inevitably meet, and she had the eerie feeling that her life would never be the same as a result.

'So when I saw you with Jamie and Lisa again, I——'

'You jumped to some very hasty conclusions!' Ginny interjected sharply, her composure torn to ribbons by her own disturbed thoughts and the way his voice sounded genuinely worried and penitent. This was a genuine, honest apology, not just a polite form of words, and she didn't know how to handle it.

'Well, what was I to think? No one had mentioned any other woman in connection with Marshall. I knew which school the children went to, so the next morning I waited some way along the route—and you came along with Jamie and Lisa. They were so obviously relaxed with you that they had to know you pretty well. And Ginny *could* be taken as being short for Ginevra.'

The wry smile that accompanied Ross's words tugged at Ginny's heart and, knowing herself to be in grave danger of making the fatal mistake of softening towards him, she forced herself to sound stiff and unyielding as she answered.

'If you'd done your spying more thoroughly, then the fact that the children were relaxed should have told you I wasn't Miss Blythe. They don't like her—and I'm sure the feeling's mutual. She's not at all the maternal type.'

'Why do you say that?'

'I've seen her with them. She doesn't want to be bothered—doesn't want them in the way. She's a society lady, is our Miss Blythe, very sleek and sophisticated, and a couple of time-consuming, messy small people don't fit with that image at all.'

Another smile threatened the control she had fought so hard to impose on herself. Warm with genuine amusement, it was wide, almost boyish, reminding her irresistibly of Jamie's face when the incident of the broken lamp had all been sorted out, and, strangely, Ross too looked as if a heavy burden had been lifted from his shoulders.

'You don't like her, do you?'

'I've only met her once,' Ginny admitted honestly. 'But, no, I didn't take to her at all—and from the things they've said, neither did Jamie and Lisa.'

The words Ross muttered were almost inaudible, impossible to catch clearly. Ginny *thought* he'd said,

'Thank heaven!' but she could see no reason for any such reaction.

A moment later Ross stood up abruptly, pushing one hand roughly through the dark silkiness of his hair, the simple movement infinitely disturbing because as Ginny's eyes followed it all she could think of was how much she would like to do just that, run her fingers through the shining strands, feel its softness under her fingertips. The urge was so strong that she had to clasp her hands tightly in her lap for fear some involuntary movement might betray her.

'I could do with a drink. How about you?'

Ginny's instinctive reaction was to shake her head. She was already so hypersensitive to everything about him, the strength of his firm body, the sound of his voice, the glowing colour of his eyes, that her nerves were strung tight as a bow-string drawn back ready to fire. Alcohol might relax her but, equally, it might intensify those feelings, loose the arrow with who knew what devastating results. But almost immediately she reconsidered, and stilled the negative movement as another thought struck her.

If alcohol might relax her, then surely it might also have the same effect on Ross? In the few days she had been in his company, never once had she seen him anything other than watchfully alert and wary, those blue eyes watching every movement. Even when he appeared at ease—as he had done a few minutes before—there was a subtle tension about the way he held himself, a tautness of muscle, like that of a jungle cat poised ready to spring. Even asleep he had been aware of the slightest movement or sound—the speed with which he had reacted to Lisa's cry proved that—and she had come to despair of finding the opportunity she needed, thinking she would never see an occasion on which his attention wasn't fully on what he was doing so that she could make her escape. But perhaps after a few drinks he would grow careless . . .

'I'd like that.' She was delighted to hear that her voice sounded calm and even, no hint of the fluttering sensation inside her ruffling its smoothness. She had thought such control would be beyond her because she was shaken to realise how, even though she was certain that, whatever his plans for Gavin, Ross would never actually harm the children, the need to escape was stronger than ever before—and not just for Jamie and Lisa's sake. She had to get away to let Gavin Marshall know where his children were, but much more than that she needed to escape for her own sake, to get away from this man who attracted and yet repelled her so strongly, a man whose motives she distrusted, whose actions she detested, but to whom she was so frighteningly vulnerable that she felt as if she were losing her grip on reality.

'I've beer—and brandy.' Ross was surveying the contents of the drinks cabinet. 'Oh, and there's some burgundy here—'

'Wine would be lovely.'

'OK, the burgundy it is. I think I'll join you. I've had a couple of shocks to the system already tonight—a dose of spirits would be the last straw.' He straightened up, the bottle in his hand. 'It's rather a large bottle,' he added drily. 'But we don't have to drink the lot.'

I certainly won't, Ginny thought. But I'll try to make sure that *you* have more than your fair share, and then we'll see what happens. She'd drink as little as she possibly could, she resolved, still not entirely sure that this was a good idea. Sharing a bottle of wine in the cosy warmth of the fire was altogether too intimate an occupation for her peace of mind. And she wished Ross wouldn't smile like that. It made her nerves quiver in response, sent a glow through her that had nothing to do with the heat of the flames.

While Ross hunted in the kitchen for the bottle-opener, Ginny tried to compose herself and force herself to think clearly. If her scheme for getting Ross drunk, or at least relaxed enough to be off his guard, was to work, she had to be completely in control. One false move could ruin everything.

Suddenly too restless to sit still any longer, she got up and prowled around the room that had become so familiar to her over the past four days. It seemed impossible that she had never known this house until now. In any other circumstances, Ross's home would have been a place in which she could have been totally comfortable and relaxed. She liked everything about it—its size, the way it was decorated, the garden she had seen from the window—but the way in which she had come to this house, and the man who owned it and her own ambiguous feelings towards him, must always come between her and that enjoyment. A book lay face-down on the windowsill and she picked it up idly, blinking in surprise as she saw the title.

What was Ross doing with a biography of Richard the Third? This was no lightweight read, either. A brief flick through the pages showed her that it was a dense, factual account with numerous footnotes and references, and the book itself was huge, inches thick and heavy enough to use as a doorstop.

Suddenly she recalled the brief glimpse she had had of the room at the opposite side of the hall, the book-shelves crammed and overflowing, the computer and word processor on the desk, the whole effect of intellectual, academic pursuits clashing violently with the image of Ross the kidnapper.

But then, Ross wasn't the usual sort of kidnapper. He had said that he had kidnapped Jamie and Lisa in revenge for the way Gavin had treated his sister—but Gavin had accused Ross of being instrumental in the break-up of his marriage by the way he had poisoned his wife's mind against her husband. She didn't know which man to believe.

But, on the evidence she had, there was only one man she *could* believe. Gavin's concern had been for his children. Ross, for all his care of them over the past few days, saw them simply as a means to an end. He had said that he had planned their abduction with a coldly meticulous care, had revealed his hatred of Gavin in those flashes of black anger that he hadn't even tried to hide. His admission of his mistake about her identity, his honest apology for getting her involved, had lulled her into a sense of false security, making her forget the ruthlessness with which he had pursued his vendetta against his brother-in-law, a vendetta in which she and the children were still hopelessly entangled, and she had no idea what Ross's ultimate aim might be.

'Here you are.'

The quiet words, the light touch on her shoulder, broke into Ginny's thoughts so abruptly that she started violently, the book falling from her hands as she swung round to face Ross, her eyes wide, dark pools of panic above her ashen cheeks. She barely saw the glass he held out to her, her attention concentrated on his face so that she saw his swift frown, the sudden darkening of those vivid blue eyes. What she was quite unprepared for was the flash of raw emotion that flared like a flame in their depths.

'Don't look at me like that!' Ross declared, his tone rough and uneven. 'For pity's sake, Ginny, I'm not going to hurt you!'

'Aren't you?' Ginny flung the words at him, the dark thoughts she had just faced still lingering in her mind like a thundercloud on the horizon.

'Dear lord, what do you think I am? No——' Ross's voice was suddenly very quiet, his eyes burningly intent on her face. 'No, Ginny, I mean you no harm. You have my word on that.'

Oh, how she wished she could believe him. She *wanted* to believe him, wanted it with a desperation that made her tremble just to think of it. His sincerity seemed as genuine as it had when he had apologised earlier, those clear eyes meeting hers without hesitation or subterfuge.

But she had to remember that other Ross, the cold, hard man she had first met. If she was tempted to forget that he existed, she had only to think of the children asleep upstairs, a small boy and girl who had been snatched away from their father, innocent victims in whatever hateful scheme this man had planned. From the back of her mind came the memory of Gavin's description of Ross as an accomplished and practised seducer, and she welcomed it gladly as it enabled her to put *this* Ross into perspective, seeing his new persona as a deliberate front, carefully assumed in order to lull her fears and suspicions.

Her eyes focusing at last on the glass in Ross's hand, Ginny snatched it from him and unthinkingly gulped down some of the rich, ruby liquid, welcoming its effect as some warmth spread through her veins, melting the ice that seemed to have formed there.

'Steady!' Ross's reproof was soft. 'You don't want to get roaring drunk.'

Right now, the thought was tempting, Ginny admitted privately. She felt as if she had been balancing on a tightrope for the past few days, never knowing if one unwary move would send her crashing to the ground, and the thought of any sort of escape from the tensions she had endured seemed infinitely welcome.

Escape! The word jolted her back to sanity with a rush as she recalled her plan to do just that. She had to get a grip on herself or she would ruin everything—and the first thing to do was to lull Ross's suspicions, make him believe that *his* plan to seduce her was working, smooth away that watchful frown from his face. With an effort she forced her mouth into a smile, though her lips felt stiff and wooden, incapable of movement.

'I was thirsty.' To her intense relief she saw the frown that darkened Ross's face lighten perceptibly, giving her the strength to go on. 'Look, why don't we sit down and relax?'

You relax, she added in her thoughts. I have no intention of doing any such thing. Please God, let this work, she prayed silently. Because if it doesn't I have no idea at all what I'm going to do!

CHAPTER EIGHT

'Why Richard the Third?'

It was the only thing Ginny could think of to ask. When they were both seated her mind had gone completely blank for a few, terrifying seconds, and she had looked desperately around the room, seeking inspiration for something that could turn the conversation into safer, trivial channels, her gaze lighting on the book, now carefully replaced on the windowsill, with a rush of relief.

'I mean, why are you reading a book about him?'

'He fascinates me and—' There was a momentary pause and, watching Ross's face intently, Ginny had the feeling that he had reconsidered what he had been about to say. 'He was a fascinating man,' he finished simply.

'You find a murderer fascinating?' The question came too sharply, revealing her inner tension too clearly.

'Murderer? He was a man of his time, he—'

'But he killed the little princes, didn't he? His own nephews—' She stopped abruptly, startled into silence by Ross's laughter.

'Don't tell me you've swallowed that old story. No one seriously believes that any more. For one thing, politically it would have been a very bad move to dispose of the princes in that way—and would a man who, from all the evidence, was devoted to his brother Edward when he was king, willingly do away with the brother's sons? After all, Richard's motto was "Loyalty Binds Me".'

Something in the way Ross spoke caught Ginny's attention.

'Loyalty's very important to you, isn't it?'

For a moment Ross looked taken aback by her question, almost as surprised as she had been to hear herself ask it, but then he nodded, his expression serious.

'Loyalty, honour, trust—call it what you will. Without it, human relationships would be non-existent. To betray a trust is one of the worst crimes anyone can commit.'

The sudden change in his tone left Ginny with the strong conviction that he was speaking from a deeply held belief. He wasn't the sort of man to make such assertions simply for effect.

Was this what Gavin Marshall had done? Had he betrayed Ross's trust in some way? If he had, then she could understand part of the savage anger that filled Ross whenever Marshall's name was mentioned—but even that didn't justify the terrible revenge he had taken.

'More wine?' Ross asked, and Ginny recognised a deliberate attempt to change the subject. She was about to say no when she realised with a distinct shock that her glass was completely empty; she had drunk the wine he had poured earlier without even being aware of it. To refuse another drink now might well make Ross suspicious, so she let him refill her glass and took a slow sip of the glowing liquid. It really was delicious, but she was going to have to take this glass much more slowly.

'I'm intrigued by this agency of yours,' Ross went on, clearly determined to avoid whatever it was that she had come close to with her talk of loyalty. 'What exactly do you do? How did you get started in the first place? No, sorry—' He laughed, seeing Ginny's bemused face and misinterpreting the reason for it. 'One question at a time, right?'

Ginny didn't know how to answer him; her mind was still full of the implications raised by his earlier comments and she found it difficult to switch from that to talking about her job. Seeing her involuntary frown, the laughter faded from Ross's eyes and his face sobered abruptly.

'I'd like to know more about you—if you don't think I'm prying.'

Ginny had thought she had seen every possible side to his character, but this was another new Ross, that hesitant, uncertain note in his voice so unlike his usual crisply confident way of speaking.

'I've lived through the past few days believing you were Ginevra Blythe, so now I find it hard to adjust to the fact that you're someone else entirely—so would you tell me something about yourself, who you really are? You can tell me to go to hell if you like,' he added, treating her to another of those disturbingly boyish smiles against which her defences were becoming steadily weaker, so that she responded more spontaneously than she had planned, her own mouth curving in response before she had time to consider whether such a reaction was wise.

'It all started by accident, really. I did a business studies course at college, but the only job I could get at first was as a secretary—temping for an agency. While I was doing that I met lots of married woman with young children who complained about the difficulties in finding reliable cleaners or childminders—that gave me the idea. I was earning quite good money as a temp, so I stashed away every penny I could and then Dad gave me a lump sum as a birthday present so I could go into business for myself. I found a small office to rent and built up a list of people who wanted to do the sort of jobs I knew these other women were looking for. At first, most of my contacts came by word of mouth, but later I invested in some pretty expensive advertising and it seems to have paid off.'

'And it's just cleaners and child minders you deal with?'

'That's how it started off. Now I have people on my books who are nannies, gardeners, even painters and decorators. We also offer a pet-sitting or house-sitting service when people go away on holiday. It—it seems to be going from strength to strength.'

Her voice jerked awkwardly as, in her enthusiasm, she looked straight into Ross's eyes, finding the warm admiration she surprised in them distinctly unsettling, and she hastily swallowed some more of her wine to ease the feeling. What would be happening at work now? she wondered. How would Carol be coping without her? The other girl was new to the job; it was only lately that the agency had begun to pay its way well enough for her to be able to afford extra help in the office.

'And what about life outside the office. Family?' There was a small but distinct pause. 'Men?'

'Mum and Dad and one sister. Dad's an accountant.'

The question about her family was easy to answer, but Ginny knew that the uncomfortable feeling in the pit of her stomach came from the fact that she had to admit, if only to herself, that apart from that one belated remembrance of him she hadn't spared Mike a thought during the time she had been with Ross. Well, that was hardly surprising, she rationalised. She had had far too much on her mind coping with each day as it came to leave her free to think of other people.

'He does the books for the agency,' she hurried on, wanting to push away the uncomfortable thought that it wasn't just her situation but Ross himself who had pushed all thoughts of Mike from her mind. 'And there's Ruth—my sister, she's married with two sons—Rory and Jason. Rory's eight and Jason nearly seven.'

'Do you see them often?'

'As often as I can. I frequently babysit so that Ruth and Sam can go out.' A warm smile lit her face. 'Though Rory strongly objects to the word *baby*sitter. He thinks he's far too big for that. Ruth calls me her menace-minder.'

Ross's chuckle was a soft, warm sound deep in his throat.

'They obviously mean a lot to you.'

'They're family,' Ginny responded simply, the words catching in her throat as the sudden realisation of how far away her family with its comfort and support was from her present, frightening situation. 'Families are important,' she added in a rush, fighting back the wave of loneliness that threatened to swamp her.

She was surprised to see Ross nodding in agreement, but then she recalled the warmth that had been in his voice when he had spoken of his mother. Would she ever be able to define the bundle of contradictions that added up to make the complex character that was Ross Hamilton?

'That explains where you get your experience in handling children,' Ross said with a smile that only aggravated her confusion.

And where do you get yours? she wanted to fling at him. How had a man like Ross come to learn the patience and tolerance he'd shown so often over the past four days?

'And men?' Ross repeated his question; evidently he had noticed the way she had sidestepped it earlier. 'Isn't there someone—'

'The imaginary fiancée?' To her consternation, Ginny found she had spoken the words out loud. The wine must be affecting her more than she had realised. Her stomach clenched nervously as she saw the way Ross's eyes narrowed.

'There isn't a real one?'

It was too late to go back now. 'Oh—no, I haven't met the right man yet.'

Haven't you? a small, unwanted voice murmured in the back of her mind, throwing her completely so that she took an unwary swallow of her wine.

'There's Mike,' she added hastily, but then something in the way Ross's face changed made her continue, 'But he's just a friend, really.'

And as she said it she knew that that was the exact truth. Mike was pleasant company, fun to be with, but if the relationship had been going anywhere she would have known it before now. There was no spark, no fire, nothing like there was with— She clamped down hard on that train of thought.

But in spite of her efforts it wouldn't be crushed. Ginny had a sudden, vivid image of the present situation as it would appear to anyone else's eyes—the two of them lounging beside the fire, a bottle of wine open between them, both of them relaxed and—yes, she admitted to herself, she, at least, felt at ease in a way she hadn't experienced since the morning Ross had exploded into her life with the force of a nuclear bomb. She *liked* being here and, what was far more destructive to her mental equilibrium, she found she was actually liking *Ross*.

'What about you?' she asked jerkily, hoping she had managed to disguise just how important she now found the question was to her.

'There's no one special.'

Was she being over-sensitive, or had there been a subtle emphasis on the last word? According to Gavin Marshall, no woman was 'special' to this man. Wasn't he likely to discard the current favourite in favour of a new interest if the opportunity presented itself?

'But I—'

'Have lots of women friends,' Ginny rushed in, unnerved by the sudden stab of pain in her heart.

There was a brief pause, then blue eyes locked with brown, Ross's expression strangely intent.

'If by "friends" you mean lovers, then no.' A muscle moved at the corner of his mouth, as if he was trying to suppress a smile as he registered Ginny's start of surprise. 'It might not be very fashionable, but I've never gone in for one-night stands or brief, meaningless relationships. I like to get to know a woman before I take her to bed.'

That electric blue gaze was mesmerising. Ginny felt it could almost draw her soul out of her body, and she suddenly knew, without any logical or rational explanation, that on this point at least Gavin hadn't been strictly truthful. But, if that was so, how much of the rest of what he had told her was untrue? She gulped down what remained of the rest of her wine, barely noticing when Ross refilled her glass.

'I understand that. I—I couldn't make love with someone I didn't know well.'

The tiny part of her brain that was still thinking rationally registered horrified shock at what she was saying, but her tongue seemed to be out of control and she couldn't stop herself from continuing. 'There has to be something very special there—that indefinable spark that makes this person so very different.'

She was lost in his eyes, adrift on a sea of feeling such as she had never experienced in her life before, Ross's silence communicating more understanding than he could ever put into words.

She had said that she had never met the right man, but why kid herself? She *had* found that someone who created that very special spark in her life. In the man before her she had found everything she could ever want—but he was quite the wrong person for her to feel that way about. Or was he? What was true and what a lie in what Gavin had told her?

'But even if that excitement is there, it's all such a risk,' she went on. 'How do you ever *know*? Most women say that they want a man who's experienced, but if he's—known—a lot of women, how can you ever be sure that he feels that special something for *you*?'

Her voice trailed off as she saw the way Ross's eyes had changed, his dilated pupils obscuring almost all the blue until it was just a narrow rim at the edge of the iris, so that they were just deep, dark pools.

'Experience isn't everything.' His voice was low and soft, so gentle it was almost a physical caress. 'If a man has any sensitivity at all, it only takes one woman to give him that. It's how he feels about someone that makes him a real lover. And, as for knowing how someone feels, that's a risk we all have to take. We can only play safe for just so long—after that we have to take a leap in the dark and pray. Ginny—' There was a new note in Ross's voice, enticing, huskily compelling, and his dark-eyed gaze shifted from her face to her mouth and then back again, holding her transfixed. 'I want very much to kiss you.'

She wanted that too, Ginny thought hazily. It wasn't wise, in fact it was downright foolish and dangerous, but none of that seemed to matter any more. She should say no, but when she tried to shake her head it wouldn't move and her dry lips wouldn't form any words of denial. When her tongue moved nervously to moisten them, she saw Ross's gaze follow the tiny movement; then, without a word, he reached out and gently took her glass from her hand, placing it carefully on the tiled hearth with his own before he leaned forward, his arm bridging the gap between their chairs as his hand cupped her cheek.

'I've wanted this from the moment I saw you,' he murmured, his voice very low. 'But I thought I'd never——'

His voice died and Ginny had a swift, overwhelming glimpse of the fire that burned in his eyes before his head moved and his mouth came down on hers.

It began as a gentle kiss, soft and infinitely tender, but within the space of a heartbeat it was as if that brief contact had created a spark that fuelled a roaring, blazing conflagration. Still with his lips on hers, Ross moved from his seat to gather her up into his arms, drawing her close against him so that she could feel the heavy, rapid thudding of his heart under her cheek as his mouth pressed down on hers, hungry, passionate, demanding.

An answering heat seemed to uncoil itself inside Ginny, sending a burning desire coursing through her veins, and her mouth opened to his, instinctively inviting, enticing. With a groan deep in his throat, Ross drew her down on to the settee, lowering her back on to the soft cushions, the hard weight of him covering her, her body glorying in the strength of his encircling arms.

She was drowning in sensation, the taste, the feel of him, the scent of his skin, and her hands moved of their own accord, sliding under the blue sweatshirt to touch the warm smoothness of his back, her fingers clenching over the powerful muscles.

'Oh, Ginny—Ginny——'

Her name was a restless, incoherent litany muttered against her skin as Ross's lips scorched a burning trail down her throat and traced the outline of the loose neck of the pyjama jacket. As Ginny stirred beneath him one leg slid between hers, the warmth of his skin reaching her through the thin cotton of the navy pyjamas.

The heat inside her had grown, building up into a raging need that rose to a crescendo of desire as the buttons on her jacket were tugged free of their fastenings, Ross's strong fingers caressing her skin, brushing the tips of her breasts with a delicacy that tantalised and tormented, making her arch her body against his. Once again that brief, featherlight caress teased her so that she moaned a faint protest and heard Ross's soft laughter.

'Is this what you want, my love?' he whispered, cupping one breast in either hand and rubbing his thumbs across their swollen peaks. 'Or this——'

His head bent, his mouth warm against her skin, the movement of his tongue across her sensitised nipples making her blood glow like liquid fire. But when his hands moved lower, sweeping over the length of her body, she tensed suddenly, a frisson of fear sweeping over her nerves. This was all so new——

Immediately Ross lifted his head, his eyes darkly serious, looking deep into hers.

'What is it, darling? Am I going too fast for you? You only have to say.'

Ginny could only shake her head mutely. Things *had* happened too fast, but she didn't want him to stop now. When Ross remained still, she used her hands to encourage him, stroking, caressing, wandering over the warm satin of his skin until, with an impatient sound deep in his throat, he shrugged himself out of his sweatshirt, the pyjama trousers following swiftly, and a wordless sigh escaped her as she felt his naked body against her own.

His caresses were less gentle now, more demanding, and Ginny felt her passion rise to meet that demand until she was strung tight as a violin-string, all fear, all thought beyond her need of him obliterated from her mind.

'Now!' a voice cried, and vaguely she realised that it was her own. But against her cheek she felt Ross shake his head.

'Not yet,' he whispered, her warm breath feathering over her skin. 'I want it to be right for you. I want this to be perfect.'

Right? Ginny thought hazily. How could it be any *more* right? How could she feel any more? But then Ross's hands touched her with delicate intimacy, his caresses creating such a maelstrom of feeling that she thought her mind might blow apart under their intensity. She barely felt his body blend with hers, knew it only as a further heightening of the sensations that she had thought could never be more exquisite, his movements making her cry out in wonder and dig her nails deep into the powerful muscles of his back. Her head was spinning; there was nothing in the world but herself and Ross and the conflagration they had lit between them.

'Ginny—my love!'

She heard her name on his lips, heard her own voice echo 'My love,' before the sensual explosion swept her into oblivion.

Very, very slowly, she came down to earth, but in Ginny's mind that was still far too soon.

'I didn't want that to end,' she murmured dreamily as the world righted itself and she came back to the realisation of Ross's arms still holding her tightly, so that she felt as well as heard the laughter that shook his body.

'That wasn't an end, my love. That was just the beginning.'

She was too tired, too perfectly happy to respond, drifting into sleep as soon as she closed her eyes. But when, some hours later, some movement or sound woke her to find herself still curled up in front of the fire, the blanket that Ross must have fetched at some point her only covering, there was no protective haze of ecstasy to shield her thoughts and prevent reality from rushing back with a force that made her feel as if a cruel, icy hand had gripped her heart.

'That wasn't an end... That was just the beginning.' Ross's words came back to haunt her, mocking her with their impossible promise of hope. There could be no beginning for herself and Ross. There was no possible future for her with him.

What had happened had changed nothing. Her eyes went to Ross's face, pillowed on his hands, his eyes tightly closed, the dark hair falling over his forehead in soft disarray, and a small, choking cry rose up in her throat. He looked so deceptively innocent and defenceless with the dark stubble shadowing his cheeks, the harsh planes of his face relaxed in sleep, that air of vulnerability made all the more poignant by the knowledge that it was just an illusion. Tears burned in Ginny's eyes wrapped her arms tightly round herself, holding back a moan of pain.

Ross had been wrong. What had happened *had* been an end, not a beginning. Beguiled by his persuasive attraction, the seductive pull of his compelling physical presence, she had abandoned her own principles and fallen completely under his spell. She had truly believed that she would never make love with any man unless there was some future in it—but what sort of a future could there be with Ross? The desire he had sparked off in her had overwhelmed her, obliterating rational thought, driving her to forget the truth. Her dismissal of Gavin's words had been intuitive, unthinking; in the cold light of day, she had to face the fact that all the evidence was to the contrary. Ross felt nothing for her; how could a man who was capable of the cold-blooded kidnapping of Jamie and Lisa, a man as eaten up with hate as he had shown himself to be, ever feel any emotion that came close to love?

She bit down hard on her lower lip as her memory denied the word 'cold-blooded', throwing up images of the night before, when Ross's blood had been every bit as hot as her own.

But then, as she sat up slowly, shivering as the cold air touched her naked skin, a new thought filled her mind, momentarily driving the pain before it. Ross was *asleep*. The moment she had longed for, prayed for, the time when for once his powerful defences were down, was within her grasp at last. And now it was so much more important, for her own sake, that she get away from him. If he would just sleep long enough for her to dress and get out of the house...

It took every ounce of determination she possessed not to leap to her feet and dash from the room, but to ease herself slowly from under the blankets, making every move as carefully as possible so as not to wake the sleeping man at her side. She took precious seconds to tuck the blanket firmly round Ross so that he wouldn't feel the loss of warmth where she had been, though her mind was crying out to her to go, get away as quickly as she could. Her action reminded her unbearably of the way Ross himself had paused to tuck Jamie in only a few hours before, the pain of the memory stabbing like the point of a white-hot knife. If only that man could have been the real Ross; how very different things might have been then.

As she moved towards the door something tangled round her feet and, looking down, she saw that it was the navy pyjama jacket, discarded in the heat of shared passion such a brief time before. She couldn't bear to remember that passion now, and with a violent, shuddering movement she kicked it away from her and fled from the room.

In the bedroom it took only seconds to pull on her clothes before she turned towards the bed, her fingers crossing unconsciously as she lifted the pillow on the side where Ross always slept. She couldn't keep back the cry of delight that sprang from her lips when she saw the bundle of keys lying on the white sheet. By an incredible stroke of luck there were not only the house keys she had expected but also an extra bonus in the shape of the keys to Ross's car. Snatching them up, she headed back towards the stairs, pausing on the landing, her eyes going to the bedroom door behind which Jamie and Lisa still slept.

No. Her decision was made almost instantly. If she woke the children now they would be confused, reluctant to move, and she couldn't afford the time it would take to reassure them, persuade them to keep quiet as they left the house. Every second was precious, and if her luck held she could find help and be back before Ross had a chance to do anything. He had looked as if he would sleep for hours yet, and he would find it difficult to move the children anywhere else without a car.

Her hands were shaking as she slid the Escort's key into the ignition, and as she did so she glimpsed a flash of white in the glove compartment. Further investigation revealed an airmail letter with an American stamp, the address on it telling her that Ross's cottage was somewhere in Nottinghamshire. Well, at least that gave her something to go on, she thought, tossing the letter aside as she started the engine.

It took a few minutes to get the Escort out of the garage, minutes that made Ginny's heart race in panic at the thought that the sound of its engine, which seemed terrifying loud in the stillness of the early morning, might wake Ross, bringing him after her just when freedom seemed so very near. But no dark figure appeared in the cottage's doorway as she swung the car out on to the road, her palms, damp with sweat, slipping on the wheel. Refusing to allow herself even one glance back at the house in which she had spent the last four days, she chose a direction at random and pressed her foot down hard on the accelerator.

CHAPTER NINE

THE small town of Boroughford was just beginning to wake up as Ginny steered the Escort into its centre. After a long debate with herself she had decided against calling in at the first house she saw and asking to be permitted to telephone the police. For one thing, she felt that the time needed to convince anyone that her plight was genuine might be more than she could afford, and for another she believed that the police themselves would be more convinced if she told her story in person. So she had followed the signposts for the market town, where she might hope to find a reasonably sized police station.

She drove down the main street slowly, looking to right and left, her whole body aching with tiredness and the tension that resulted from her refusal to allow herself to think about the man she had left behind her, so that when she saw a familiar face for a moment she thought it was a delusion, the stresses she had endured making her eyes play tricks on her. But a swift glance in the rearview mirror told her she hadn't been mistaken and, thankful that there was no one behind her, she swerved sharply to bring the car in to the kerb and slammed the brakes on hard.

It *was* Gavin Marshall. There was no mistaking the tall, immaculately suited man who stood on the steps of an expensive-looking hotel, his fair hair gleaming in the mellow autumn sunlight. Ginny's hand was on the door, but even as she moved to open it something held her back, and she sank back in her seat again, watching Marshall through the mirror.

What was wrong with her? *Why* had she hesitated? For days, all she had thought of was escaping from Ross, finding Gavin Marshall and returning Jamie and Lisa to his safekeeping—so why was she sitting here, frozen in her seat, when the achievement of all her aims was so very close?

Because she couldn't do it. The answer came with frightening speed and clarity, even as she shook her head in bewilderment at her own decision. And now all the feelings she had pushed out of her mind during the headlong journey away from the cottage swept over her like a tidal wave until she felt she was drowning in them.

Gavin Marshall, the children's father, was only yards away from her, and yet she was as incapable of getting out of the car and going to him as she would have been if the short distance between them had been a vast, unbridgeable chasm. If she told Marshall what had happened, revealed to him how close he was to his children and the man who had abducted them, he would inevitably head straight for the nearest police station and ask for help to rescue Jamie and Lisa and bring their kidnapper to justice—and it was that last fact that deprived her of the ability to move.

But wasn't that exactly what she had planned to do herself? Hadn't she driven here with the one idea of reporting everything to the police? With a sense of despair, Ginny faced the fact that, if Jamie and Lisa were to be returned to their father, that was the only thing she could do.

Her eyes went back to the smartly dressed man on the hotel steps. Something was wrong; every instinct told her so. She had imagined Gavin Marshall looking pale and distraught, eaten up with worry about the fate of his son and daughter, but this man showed no sign of any such anxiety. Instead, he was smiling broadly as he chatted to the woman at his side.

Not Ginevra Blythe, Ginny noted automatically, but a tall, dark, strikingly dressed woman whose pale face had a hauntingly familiar beauty that made Ginny wonder where she had seen it before. Perhaps in some newspaper or magazine, she reflected as a taxi pulled up outside the hotel and Marshall helped the woman into it, standing back to watch the car drive out of sight before giving a quick, satisfied-looking nod and turning to go back inside.

'Now!' Ginny muttered, trying to spur herself into action. But the word reverberated in her mind, bringing devastating echoes of that same syllable uttered in such totally different circumstances, in a voice shaken with fevered passion, so that her resolve deserted her once more as her inner conflict threatened to tear her mind in two.

She knew what she must do—knew the only right thing was to get out of the car and find Gavin Marshall and tell him everything. He was Jamie and Lisa's father—their *father*, she repeated, the word firming her resolution so that at last she was able to open the car door and step out on to the pavement. How she felt was irrelevant. What Ross had done was wrong, and now she had a chance to put things right.

Bitter tears stung her eyes as she walked towards the hotel's reception desk. It didn't matter how she rationalised it, how many times she told herself she was doing the right thing, it still seemed so *wrong*, as if she was betraying Ross, so that it was a struggle to meet the receptionist's enquiring gaze.

'Do you have a Mr Gavin Marshall staying here?'

It was as she spoke that an idea came to her, bringing with it a tiny flicker of hope that she had found a way to do right by the children and their father and yet not betray Ross—because no amount of argument could persuade her that it would be anything other than a betrayal.

'Could I leave a note for him?'

The other woman's frown was puzzled. Clearly, she couldn't understand why anyone should want to leave a note when Gavin Marshall was there, in the hotel, and could easily be contacted direct. But she pushed note-paper and an envelope towards Ginny and turned to answer the telephone which had been ringing insistently.

Ginny wrote swiftly, her hand shaking so that it was a struggle to form the words clearly.

'Mr Marshall, Jamie and Lisa are alive and well. They can be found at——'

She hesitated, biting the end of the pen as she tried to recall the address she had seen on the letter in the car. For one desperate moment she couldn't bring it to mind, and her hand clenched around the pen until her fingers ached. But then, with a rush of relief, she suddenly had a clear mental picture of the airmail envelope and the writing on it, and she bent over the page again.

She was uncertain whether to sign the letter or not, but finally, with a sigh, added her name. Gavin must know that she had disappeared with the children. He might have doubts about an anonymous note, but surely he would act on her instructions without hesitation? Folding the note, she stuffed it hastily into the envelope and sealed it.

'Could you give this to Mr Marshall—but not im-mediately. If you could wait, say——'

She consulted her watch. The journey from the cottage had taken just over a quarter of an hour. Two minutes to read the note, five at the most to contact the police if he wanted to—What *had* Gavin been doing in Boroughford? Had he or the police finally tracked Ross down? And, if that was the case, why wasn't he at the cottage already? She didn't know, but she could only be grateful that this was the way things had worked out. Her plan depended on Gavin reaching Ross's house some time after she did.

'Fifteen minutes—no more—then give it to him, I'd be most grateful.'

The receptionist looked as if she believed this strange woman had gone out of her mind, and she handled the envelope as if she thought it might contain a letter-bomb. 'I'll see that he gets it.'

But Ginny barely heard her; already she was hurrying across the foyer, breaking into a run as soon as she was back in the street.

Once in the car, she had to control the urge to put her foot down on the accelerator until she was out of Boroughford. It wouldn't do to be had up for speeding now, when all she wanted was to avoid the police at all costs. On the outward journey she had refused to let herself think, forcing herself to concentrate on finding her way through the winding lanes and country roads, but now she was unable to impose any such control, and her mind had free range to torment her with doubts and unhappy thoughts.

Her decision had been made on impulse. She had no idea if her plan would actually work, but she *had* to try it. If she told Ross that she had informed Gavin of his whereabouts, that Marshall and, possibly, the police were on their way to the cottage right this minute—as they would be by the time she spoke to Ross—then surely he would see that the only thing he could do was to hand the children over to her and get away?

But wasn't she taking a very great risk? Was the man who had planned this kidnapping with such cold calculation likely to abandon his plan of revenge just like that, with no return for his efforts? And what if he became violent? She wouldn't stand a chance against his strength if he used force against her. The car veered sharply as Ginny's hands clenched on the wheel.

No. With a shuddering sigh she pulled herself together. Ross wasn't a violent man. No one who had cared for the children as he had, who had soothed Lisa after her nightmare in that gentle, tender way—even allowing for the appalling lie he had told her about her mother—could be naturally a man of violence. But, just the same, she would stand well away from him when she told him. If she kept out of his reach——

A sob choked her as her mind threw up a vivid memory of a pair of strong arms enfolding her, the warmth of a hard, male body against her own. How could she keep her distance when even now, remembering, her whole body ached for that contact once again? If she felt like this now, how would she cope when she saw him? She would want him to touch her, want his arms round her, but now and for ever she would have to keep him at arm's length, both physically and emotionally, and she didn't know if she could do it.

'I could never make love with someone I didn't know.'

Her own words, spoken so naïvely in the darkness of the night, came back to haunt her. She had declared them so confidently, and yet Ross had only to kiss her and she was lost, drowning in a boiling sea of sensation that made a nonsense of her conviction.

She could take the easy way out, blame it on the wine, tell herself that the alcohol had affected her judgement, but in her heart she knew it wasn't true. She was stone-cold sober this morning, her judgement as cool and clear as she could wish, and still she couldn't make herself want things to have been otherwise. Given half a chance, she would do it all again. But she wasn't going to get that chance, and in that fact lay her one regret.

The cottage was in sight now, standing square and solid at the side of the road, and pain ripped through her at the sight of it, the four days she had spent there seeming like a fleeting idyll, a moment suspended out of time. During those days she hadn't seen them like that, had thought only of escape, of getting away, but now she wished she could have that time again, time to be with Ross, to see him, talk to him, to——

She swung the car to the side of the road and stopped, breathing rapidly. To *love* him! There was no escaping the word, it seemed etched into her brain in fiery letters. She loved Ross, had given her heart to him in the short space of time she had known him.

She *hadn't* gone against her deeply held belief that you had to know someone before you could love them. It was said that you had to live with a person before you could really know them, and in the time she had spent with Ross she had learned a great deal about him. She had come to admire his clear, capable mind, his patience and tolerance, his gentle handling of the children, the tenderness and understanding he had shown them and— her hands clenched on the steering wheel—herself. When Ross had made love to her he had been as patient and considerate of her feelings as any lover could ever be, holding back in spite of the urgency of his own desire in order to make sure that she experienced pleasure too.

What was it Ross had called falling in love? A leap in the dark. Well, she had made that leap, but it seemed she had only landed at the bottom of a dark chasm filled with rocks and thorns. Ross was everything she had ever wanted in a man, but what he had done would always come between them.

She didn't want to go any further. All she wanted to do was to stay here for ever, with that final parting that she knew must come still in the future so that Ross was still, in some small way, a part of her life. But time wouldn't stand still. The receptionist must have given her letter to Gavin by now, and she had to give Ross as much time as possible to get away. Her heart aching, she reached forward to start the engine again.

As she rounded the final bend that led to the cottage, Ginny's heart seemed to stop as she saw a taxi pulling away from the cottage gate. Had Ross got away with the children, after all? But there wasn't a telephone in the cottage, so how could he have contacted anyone?

Her mouth dry, she watched as the other car turned and headed back towards her, only breathing again when she saw that the driver was the only person in it.

She parked the Escort some yards from the cottage, not wanting the sound of its engine to alert Ross to her arrival. Her legs felt like lead as she walked towards the gate, her approach to the house hidden by the thick beech hedge which enclosed it.

'I'm sorry I couldn't come to meet you but I—had a problem with the car.'

Ginny's heart lurched as she recognized Ross's voice, its tone warm and gentle, immediately reviving tormenting memories of the way he had used just that tone to her only a few hours before. He was in the garden, only a few feet away from her. But who was he talking to? Not the children, obviously. Moving as silently as possible, she edged closer.

'That doesn't matter.' It was a woman's voice, soft and low. 'What does matter is that I'm here at last. Oh,

Ross, you can't imagine how I've longed for this moment!'

Ginny heard the words through the buzzing haze that filled her mind, and the world threatened to spin out of focus as she recognised the woman who had been standing on the hotel steps with Gavin Marshall. What was *she* doing here?

Blinking hard to clear her blurred eyes, Ginny forced herself to look at the couple standing only a few feet away from her, totally unaware of her presence behind the hedge. A queasy, sick sensation started up inside her stomach as she saw how Ross's arm was around the woman's waist, the two dark heads so very close together.

'You saw Marshall?'

'I've come straight from him——'

The rest of the woman's words faded as the situation became suddenly blindingly clear. Ross had said that he'd done nothing to contact the children's father—but he hadn't needed to because this woman had carried out that part of the plan for him. *She* had been the go-between, negotiating with Marshall for the children's re-lease, and clearly those negotiations had just been com-pleted—and successfully too, if the smile that lit her face was anything to go by. And Gavin Marshall had ap-peared unworried—because he knew that within a very short time his son and daughter would be returned to him!

But what was this woman to Ross? Ginny had thought that she was beyond feeling any further shock, but when the woman lifted her left hand and placed it on Ross's arm she saw the thick gold ring that flashed in the sun-light and doubled up in anguish, feeling as if her heart had just been wrenched into tiny, bleeding pieces.

Ross had said that there was no one special in his life and she had *believed* him! What a blind, deluded fool she had been! Burning tears seared her eyes, blinding her so that she didn't see the broken branch at her feet. The crack as she stood on it sounded like gunfire in the still quiet of the morning. Dimly she saw Ross's head swing round sharply.

'Ginny!'

She was beyond trying to interpret his tone, could think of nothing but getting away, running as far as she could and then hiding to lick her wounds in private like some hunted animal. But Ross moved faster than she could think; her arm was caught in a grip that she hadn't the strength to break, and she was dragged, stumbling and resisting furiously, on to the lawn where the other woman still stood.

'Ross, who is this?' The dark woman's eyes were wide with confusion.

'Someone I met—a friend——'

He seemed at a loss as to how to describe her, and no wonder, Ginny thought, a bitter taste burning her mouth. How *do* you describe to your wife the woman you kidnapped and then seduced? Disgust combined with despair in an explosive mixture.

'I'm no friend of yours!' she flung at Ross, spitting the words out in her pain.

The blue eyes were very dark, and if she hadn't known better she could have sworn that a shadow of her own devastating loss clouded them.

'Not a friend, then,' he said, his voice totally devoid of expression. 'But someone I have to talk to.'

'We've done all the talking we'll ever do! I have nothing to say to you!'

'Perhaps not, but I have things I want to explain to you. Lissa—' He turned to the dark-haired woman standing silently at his side. 'Can you give me ten minutes alone with Ginny? Why don't you go inside? They're in the living-room,' he added as her eyes, blue like his, went to his face in evident confusion.

The woman's smile erased every trace of doubt from her face, and Ginny had to bite her lip hard against the moan of anguish that almost escaped her at the sight of her all too evident happiness.

'Now.' Ross turned to her as Lissa moved away. 'I know you don't want to talk——'

'You're damn right I don't!'

Pain stabbed deep inside her as Ross's lips twitched in response to that 'damn'. She didn't want to remember the way he had teased her, didn't want to think of how it had been.

'There's nothing you can say that'll change anything! You used me—lied to me—seduced me!'

'No——' Ross began, but Ginny rushed on, not giving him a chance to speak.

'What happened?' Bitter loathing thickened her voice. 'Did you get frustrated after four nights without a woman in your bed? Couldn't you even go without that long so that you had to find someone naïve, someone gullible enough to fall for your charms? What a fool I was! "There's no one special."' She quoted his words savagely. '"I don't go in for one-night stands or brief, meaningless relationships." So tell me, what do you call a quick fling with someone who just happens to be available when your wife's not around?'

'My——'

Ross pushed a hand roughly through his hair and, despairingly, Ginny was unable to prevent her eyes from following the movement, unable to force away the memory of how it had felt to lace her fingers in that dark softness.

'Ginny, I think there's something you ought to see. Come with me—please.'

She wanted to dig her heels in and refuse to move, wanted to scream at him that she wasn't going anywhere with him, but those compelling blue eyes held her own pain-shadowed brown ones so that she was unable to say a word or make a move to resist as he took her hand and led her gently towards the cottage.

In the hall, he paused outside the living-room door.

'All I want you to do is to go in here,' he said, his voice softly persuasive. 'After that, if you still hate me, then I'll let you go. But do this for me, Ginny—*please*.'

She didn't want to go into that room, didn't want to face the heartbreaking memories the sight of it would bring, but it would have taken a far harder heart than she possessed to resist the appeal in his face and voice, and so, moving like an automaton, she opened the door.

She didn't know what she had expected, but the sight that met her eyes drove every thought from her mind. The woman Ross had called Lissa sat on the settee with Jamie and Lisa at either side of her. The woman's arms were round the children, tears flowing unrestrainedly down her cheeks, and Jamie and Lisa were clinging to her as if they never wanted to let go.

'Lissa.' Ross's voice sounded husky and strained. 'Would you please tell Ginny who you are?'

But before the woman had time to speak, Jamie had looked up and seen Ginny standing frozen in the doorway.

'Ginny!' His face was just one bright glow of ecstasy. 'Ginny, look! My mummy's come back!'

My mummy! Ginny's head reeled so violently that she swayed on her feet and might have fallen if Ross's arms hadn't come round her from behind, supporting her. But Gavin Marshall had said——

She twisted round to stare into Ross's quietly watchful face and, accurately interpreting the question in her eyes, he nodded, his mouth tightening grimly.

'I know what Marshall told you, but it's all a pack of lies.'

'Gavin and I were divorced three years ago,' Lissa's quiet voice put in. 'Our marriage was a mistake from the start. Ross saw that, but I——' She lifted her hands in a gesture that dismissed the details as irrelevant. 'After the divorce I was given custody of the children. Gavin was never a very enthusiastic father; I wanted children, he didn't. He loved his work, making more money always came first, and when we separated he rarely saw them or gave any indication of even caring what happened to them. But then I met another man, an American over here on business. We fell in love, got married—and I went back to the States with him, taking Jamie and Lisa with me.'

In her mind Ginny could hear Gavin Marshall's voice saying, 'The children have been living in America for the last couple of years,' and she remembered how his tone had struck her as rather odd at the time.

'Gavin's attitude changed dramatically then. From being totally unconcerned, he suddenly became intensely interested in the children. I think he was just plain jealous and possessive; he couldn't bear the idea of another man being a father to his children, even though he had never wanted to fill that role. He tried everything he could to stop me taking them to America, and when that didn't work he resorted to threats, said he'd take them away from me and I'd never see them again.'

Lissa's tears had dried now and her voice was low but calm.

'One day he came to visit. That was so unusual that I should have been suspicious but, foolishly, I wasn't.

He wanted to take Jamie and Lisa to the zoo, and I could see no reason to say no. He never came back.' Her voice shook on the words. 'That was six months ago. I haven't seen them since—until now.'

'Uncle Ross said my mummy was coming soon,' Lisa put in innocently, completely unaware of the effect her words were having on Ginny.

'Ginny.' Ross's voice was low and intense. 'Alicia is my sister, not my wife.'

My *sister*. It was slowly dawning on Ginny's shell-shocked mind just what all this meant to *her*.

'When Gavin took the children, we knew he'd bring them back to England eventually,' Lissa's voice took up the story again. 'That's where my kid brother here came into things.'

She turned a warm look on Ross, her eyes—Ross's eyes, Ginny now saw—glowing with happiness.

'He's been trying to find Gavin ever since he disappeared, and a few days ago he tracked him down to Epton. He rang me at once to let me know he'd found Jamie and Lisa and to plan our next move. My instructions were to do nothing until I got here. I'd planned to try talking to Gavin, see if we could work out some sort of compromise, but I couldn't get a seat on a plane for four days and Ross wasn't prepared to wait that long— snatching the children back was all his idea.'

'I wanted Marshall to have a taste of his own medicine,' Ross growled. 'I know what you went through, and when I saw the children everything else just went out of my mind. All I wanted was to get them back. The information I'd been able to gather made it only too plain that Gavin hadn't changed. He was at work all day and out with his new lover every evening. He didn't want Jamie and Lisa for themselves but to hurt you—so I made a move.'

Ross's words, though they weren't addressed to her, stung like a bitter reproach. She had believed Ross was using the children, but in fact it had been Gavin, their own father, who had been doing that.

'You always were an impulsive, headstrong creature,' his sister laughed. 'Leaping in without any forethought and to hell with the consequences.'

Ginny's legs felt weak beneath her as Lissa's comment echoed Ross's declaration that 'we have to take a leap in the dark.' She had done just that, rushing headlong into love—but what about Ross? She knew now that he wasn't the cold, callous man she had believed him to be, knew that none of what Gavin had said was true, but how did he feel about her?

With a sense of shock she realised that Ross still held her, his arms warm and firm about her waist, and she didn't know whether to stay where she was or to try to pull away.

'I never believed that——' Ross's eyes flicked to Jamie and Lisa, and he hastily amended what he had been about to say. 'That Gavin would listen to reason——'

He broke off abruptly as Ginny's hand went to her mouth in shock.

'What is it?'

'I told Gavin that the children are here!' Ginny cried shakenly. 'I should have thought of it before. Ross——'

'It's all right,' Ross soothed her gently. 'Lissa's already seen Gavin.'

Only then did Ginny remember that Ross's sister had been at the hotel with her ex-husband.

'When I had the children safe, the first thing I did was to ring Lissa and say I was bringing them here— That was when you were out for the count.' Ross's expression was wryly apologetic. 'I was quite prepared to leave Gavin to stew, but my sister's too soft-hearted.'

'I contacted Gavin and asked if we could meet to talk things out,' Lissa put in. 'I told him I was coming to England and arranged a meeting in Boroughford. I couldn't have lived the rest of my life always looking over my shoulder, never knowing if Gavin would try to take the children again. I met him last night, and it seems he's had second thoughts about everything. I think he found having Jamie and Lisa with him more difficult than he'd ever imagined, and his new fiancée hasn't taken too kindly to the idea of an instant family. She's given him an ultimatum—the children or her. My husband wants to adopt Jamie and Lisa as his own, and when I was able to offer the added inducement of never having to pay any maintenance ever again if he let me keep the children, he very soon came round.'

'I hope Miss Blythe finds the deal satisfactory.' Ross's blue eyes were hard and cold, but they softened as his gaze went to the group on the settee. 'Personally, I think you got the better half of the bargain.'

'There's one thing I don't understand.' Lissa's frown was puzzled. 'How did Ginny get involved in all this?'

Ginny tensed in Ross's arms, her breathing shallow with nerves as she waited for Ross's reply.

'That was my fault—I thought she was Gavin's fiancée.'

'Ouch!' Lissa's eyes went to Ginny's. 'I bet he gave you a rough time because of that. I know my brother— he always puts on the tough macho act when he's worried or unsure of himself.'

Ross, unsure of himself? Ginny's mind went winging back over the past few days, reviewing events and reconsidering them in this new light.

'I probably—' she began, but was unable to go on as her words drew those vivid eyes to her and she was shocked to see how Ross's face had changed, suddenly taut and strained as he moved at last, his hand leaving her waist to link with hers, enclosing it firmly.

'If you'll excuse us, Lissa, Ginny and I have some serious talking to do.'

His sister barely saw them go, her attention concentrated on the children once again.

Ross led Ginny out into the garden, pausing near the spot where she had first seen him with Lissa and turning to take her other hand in his, his face soberly intent.

'I want you to tell me something. I know you thought I was a genuine kidnapper—I wanted you to believe that because I thought you were Ginevra, that spoilt madam I'd heard about. I didn't even want to like you and I thought you were in love with Gavin—that even if I told you the truth you wouldn't believe me and you'd take his side——' He broke off abruptly, shaking his head slightly as if that had not been what he had meant to say. 'What I need to know is why you came back.'

That 'need' made a tiny flame of hope flare in Ginny's bruised heart. Was there something behind it, something she had thought lost to her forever when she had believed that Lissa was Ross's wife? Her brown eyes met his searching blue ones steadily as she answered, her voice low but firm. There could be no other answer but the truth.

'I'd planned to tell you I'd let Gavin know where you were. I left a note for him at his hotel, but I asked the receptionist to wait fifteen minutes before she gave it to him. I thought that would give me time to get here and warn you.'

'Warn me?' The speed with which the question came fanned the tiny flame to a golden glow that eased the ache from her heart. 'Why would you want to warn me?'

'I wanted to give you a chance to get away. I felt sure Gavin would go to the police and——'

Her voice failed her as she saw the flash of emotion that made his eyes gleam like brilliant jewels.

'Even though you believed I was all sorts of a bastard, you were still prepared to do that? *Why*, Ginny?'

There was no mistaking the raw note in his voice that revealed how much her answer meant to him. It told her everything she needed to know, but her heart was pounding so violently that she couldn't find the breath to speak.

'Why did you do it?' Ross prompted urgently.

'Because I love you.'

She got no chance to expand on the simple statement as she was pulled close to him, his arms coming round her, holding her tight against him, and after all her heartsearching and doubt, and the shock of the truth, it was like coming into a safe harbour after a violent storm. She felt warm and secure and totally at peace.

'And I love you, my darling girl.' Ross's voice was rough and thick with emotion. 'I think I fell head over heels for you the moment I saw you. When you got out of your car and came towards me, all I could think was that you were the most gloriously beautiful woman I'd ever seen in my life. But then Jamie called you Ginny, apparently confirming my suspicions that you were Gavin's fiancée. I was furious to think that he'd got to you first—when I hadn't even known you'd existed.'

Ross's hand stroked Ginny's cheek, sliding under her chin to lift her face towards his, his eyes burning down into hers.

'I think I went a little crazy.' His laugh was uncertain, shaken. 'As Lissa says, I have a tendency to rush in where angels fear to tread. At that moment I didn't care what I'd heard about Gavin's redhead, I just wanted to touch you, talk to you. I didn't care if it meant risking my whole plan. I knew I had to get Jamie and Lisa away, someone could have come along at any moment, but I didn't want to leave you because if I did I might never see you again. Then you fell and knocked yourself out.'

His gaze went to Ginny's jaw where the mark of the bruise was now almost non-existent, and guilt and regret shadowed the brightness of his eyes.

'I felt lousy when that happened—but at the same time I felt fate was on my side. I couldn't leave you in case you'd really hurt yourself, and that gave me a genuine excuse to take you with me. But I'll never forgive myself for letting that happen.'

Ginny reached up a hand and gently smoothed the lines of strain from his face.

'It was an accident. You mustn't blame yourself,' she murmured reassuringly; then, when it was clear that his doubts still lingered, she added with a teasing smile, 'At least I'll be able to tell people that when we met I was knocked for six—quite literally.'

That was better. The cloud that had darkened his face had lightened, and he managed a rather rueful smile.

'My concern for you wasn't the only reason I took you with me. I wanted to get you away from Gavin—permanently. The more I saw of you, the harder I found it to believe that you'd actually been taken in by a man like him, that you could ever have agreed to marry him, but you were always so concerned about him that I thought perhaps you really loved him, and I didn't know how to get the truth through to you. I wanted you to know about the Gavin I knew, to warn you against the sort of person I knew he was—but I had no way of proving anything. So I thought the best thing to do was to wait until Lissa got here and let her tell you the whole story. But then last night—this morning—you told me you weren't Ginevra Blythe at all and——'

He didn't complete the sentence, but Ginny had a vivid mental image of his face when she had told him who she really was, and knew that he did not have to go on. She could imagine only too well how he had felt.

'After that I was determined to tell you everything, but you were as jumpy as a nervous cat and I didn't think you'd listen until you had calmed down, so I suggested a drink, thinking it might relax you so that at least you'd give me a chance to explain. But my self-control isn't as strong as I thought it was—at least, not where you're concerned. I couldn't wait until I'd told you—I just had to kiss you right there and then—'

The bright blue eyes had darkened until they were almost all black, and his voice had deepened, becoming rough-edged with desire.

'As I have to now,' he whispered huskily.

His kiss was long and deep and passionate, igniting a flame in Ginny's heart that burned away every last shred of pain and doubt. She had taken a leap in the dark, but she had landed safely, finding her future on the way.

At long last Ross lifted his head, looking deep into Ginny's glowing brown eyes.

'Ginny, my love, this isn't the way I planned it.' His smile was the lop-sided, boyish grin she had found so appealing from the very beginning. 'But, impulsive as always, I just can't wait any longer. Will you marry me, my darling?'

The answer burned on her tongue, but with a mischievous glance from under her lashes she said instead, 'What way *had* you planned it?'

Impatience showed clearly on Ross's face, but he bore with her teasing good-humouredly.

'Last night—when I'd told you everything—I meant to do it all properly, go down on one knee——'

He broke off, seeing Ginny's eyes on the ground.

'If that's what you want——'

'No, you idiot!' Laughing, Ginny caught hold of him as he made a move as if to kneel. 'The lawn's terribly muddy after all the rain. I'll let you off the traditional proposal scene—and, yes,' she added in a rush, seeing his eyes and unable to keep him waiting any longer. 'Yes, yes, yes—I'll marry you.'

'Do you realise something?' she said a long time later, when she emerged from another breathtaking embrace. 'I've said I'll marry you, but I don't even know what you do—when you're not kidnapping children and your future wife, that is.'

Ross's laughter was a rich, warm sound that sent her heart soaring.

'After the brigand act, I'm afraid the reality's going to be rather a let-down. I'm a historian—a university lecturer, to be precise—but this year I'm doing research which I hope will turn into a book.' The look he shot her was filled with dry humour. 'Do you think you could settle for being an academic's wife instead of a gangster's moll?'

Joy bubbled up inside Ginny, escaping in a wide, ecstatic smile.

'I'll have a *damn* good try,' she laughed, lifting her face once more for his kiss.

'Mummy, why is Uncle Ross kissing Ginny?' a clear young voice demanded. Unobserved, Lissa and the children had come out into the garden.

'Uncle Ross is kissing Ginny because he loves her,' Ross answered, never taking his eyes from Ginny's face.

'And you'd better get used to calling her Auntie Ginny from now on, because that's what she'll be when she and I are married.'

'Oh, *great*!' Lisa jumped up and down in excitement. 'Can I be a bridesmaid?'

'Of course you can,' Ginny assured her happily. She had come to love Lisa and Jamie, and was thrilled to think that they would now be part of her family, too. They would always be very special to her, even when she and Ross had children of their own—and Ross would want children as much as she did; after seeing him with his nephew and niece, she was sure of that.

'And when is the wedding to be?' Lissa's resigned tone revealed that she fully expected the answer Ross gave her.

'Just as soon as it can possibly be arranged. As you know, sister dear, I'm a creature of impulse, always rushing headlong into impetuous action—but this time——'

His eyes held Ginny's, his love burning bright and clear in them for anyone to see.

'This has got to be the best decision I've ever made.'

And as she returned his smile Ginny knew that, for both of them, the leap they had made had not been into the dark at all, but into the bright, shining light.

Harlequin Presents®

Coming Next Month

#1271 THE WAYWARD BRIDE Daphne Clair
Pierce Allyn claims that Trista Vandeleur is a spoiled tease. Trista believes that Pierce is using her to further his career. With misgivings, they decide to marry. Then, torn by unanswered questions, each waits for the other to tell the truth.

#1272 THE POWER AND THE PASSION Emma Darcy
Her father's warning to steer clear of the dark disturbing tycoon Danton Fayette just seems to rouse Bernadette's instinct to meet the challenge. Determined to prove her father wrong, she knows she'll somehow have to fight her attraction to Danton.

#1273 BRIDE FOR A PRICE Stephanie Howard
Olivia is shattered to learn her stepfather's will left the family business in the hands of arrogant Matthew Jordan. Olivia sets out to reclaim it for her young brother's heritage, hoping that the price Matthew demands is one that she can pay....

#1274 A SPECIAL ARRANGEMENT Madeleine Ker
Romy discovers arranged marriages still exist when Xavier de Luca blackmails her. He wants heirs for his Sicilian estate—in return he'll save Romy's father from bankruptcy. Romy's feelings for Xavier are so extreme she doubts she can cope with such an arrangement.

#1275 MAN ON THE MAKE Roberta Leigh
Mark Raynor doesn't want to play nursemaid to a poor little rich girl—Charlotte Beauville doesn't want Mark's disapproving presence spoiling her fun. But she gradually comes to realize that she can trust Mark with her life!

#1276 LOVE IN A SPIN Mary Lyons
Stephanie thinks she's put the past behind her, making a contented life for herself and her young son Adam in the Cotswold village. Then Maxim Tyler moves to the manor house in the village, and the memories—and distrust—come flooding back.

#1277 FLY LIKE AN EAGLE Sandra Marton
Peter Saxon shatters Sara's peaceful life when he makes off with jewels he's being paid to guard—and takes Sara as hostage! She knows she should try to escape, turn him in—but finds herself wanting to believe he's innocent.

#1278 WISH ON THE MOON Sally Wentworth
Skye is delighted at the chance of going to the Bahamas to be bridesmaid at her cousin Jodi's wedding. Her delight changes to horror, however, when she realizes she's fallen in love with Thane Tyson—for he's the prospective groom!

Available in June wherever paperback books are sold, or through Harlequin Reader Service:

In the U.S.
901 Fuhrmann Blvd.
P.O. Box 1397
Buffalo, N.Y. 14240-1397

In Canada
P.O. Box 603
Fort Erie, Ontario
L2A 5X3

Indulge a Little
Give a Lot

A LITTLE SELF-INDULGENCE CAN DO
A WORLD OF GOOD!

Last fall readers indulged themselves with fine
romance and free gifts during the Harlequin®/
Silhouette® "Indulge A Little—Give A Lot"
promotion. For every specially marked book
purchased, 5¢ was donated by Harlequin/
Silhouette to Big Brothers/Big Sisters Pro-
grams and Services in the United States and
Canada. We are pleased to announce that your
participation in this unique promotion resulted in a total contribution of *$100,000.*

*

*Watch for details on Harlequin® and Silhouette®'s
next exciting promotion in September.*

A BIG SISTER
can take her places

She likes that. Her Mom does too.

BIG BROTHERS/BIG SISTERS AND HARLEQUIN

Harlequin is proud to announce its official sponsorship of Big Brothers/Big Sisters of America. Look for this poster in your local Big Brothers/Big Sisters agency or call them to get one in your favorite bookstore. Love is all about sharing.

BB/BS-1A

Have You Ever Wondered If You Could Write A Harlequin Novel?

Here's great news—Harlequin is offering a series of cassette tapes to help you do just that. Written by Harlequin editors, these tapes give practical advice on how to make your characters—and your story—come alive. There's a tape for each contemporary romance series Harlequin publishes.

Mail order only

All sales final

TO: *Harlequin Reader Service*
Audiocassette Tape Offer
P.O. Box 1396
Buffalo, NY   14269-1396

I enclose a check/money order payable to HARLEQUIN READER SERVICE® for $9.70 ($8.95 plus 75¢ postage and handling) for EACH tape ordered for the total sum of $_____*
Please send:

☐ Romance and Presents   ☐ Intrigue
☐ American Romance   ☐ Temptation
☐ Superromance   ☐ All five tapes ($38.80 total)

Signature_____
                                                    (please print clearly)
Name:_____

Address:_____

State:_____ Zip:_____

*Iowa and New York residents add appropriate sales tax.

                                                         AUDIO-H